Someplace Better

by
Roy LeBlanc

ISBN: 978-1-7349226-4-6

This book is printed on acid-free paper.

Printed in the United States of America

DESMOND DUPREE WAS TORN BETWEEN two exciting career opportunities: work as a Wall Street investment banker or fly Navy fighter jets. His two degrees from Tulane University in math and economics would open doors. Not quiet or shy, Desmond was determined to do exciting things. Naval aviation offered him a spot in the next flight training class aboard the USS *Theodore Roosevelt*, a carrier group based in Norfolk, Virginia. Desmond held out, optimistically waiting on Waterman Securities' elusive Wall Street offer. He decided to pursue investment banking because he wanted to know what it was like to have financial security. Desmond was tired of being poor.

The New Orleans office of Waterman Securities (WS) received 150 résumés each month, yet they only hired six recruits a year. Desmond called Mr. Nick Brandages, the WS manager, for the fourth time, requesting yet another meeting. "Mr. Brandages, can we meet for breakfast tomorrow morning?" he asked.

They met at the Intercontinental Hotel across the street from the WS office in downtown New Orleans. Mr. Brandages wore expensive three-piece suits, had perfect posture, and always had the tip of a silk handkerchief extending from his jacket pocket, matching the color of his tie. An old-fashioned pocket watch was connected to a gold chain that threaded between buttonholes in his vest. A fob made of gold and diamonds was attached to the other end of the chain. His thick gray hair was perfectly in place. He smiled confidently.

Mr. Brandages' regal appearance was in sharp contrast to Desmond's department store suit, discount tie, and vinyl shoes. Desmond did not order anything to eat or drink. He was too nervous. "I don't want to seem pushy or out of line, but I need an answer. Will

I receive a job offer from Waterman Securities?" Desmond found the courage to ask.

Mr. Brandages studied Desmond. He smiled slightly and nodded his head. "I decided to hire you during our first meeting. I have been waiting for you to close the deal! You start next week," he said. "Now relax, eat something, and start calling me Mr. Nick."

He explained the federal license requirements, including the Series 7 and Series 63 exams, that Desmond would need to obtain. The Series 7 exam had to be taken successfully on the first attempt with a minimal passing score of 70. "If you are not serious enough about your career to study and pass on the first try, then we don't need you, but don't worry, you will pass," Mr. Nick explained.

Desmond especially liked the fact that the Waterman training program required a month in New York. He had not been out of New Orleans much, except for family vacations to Pensacola and a few trips to Atlanta. Desmond had never been on an airplane.

Mr. Brandages was a great judge of talent and looked for it in the most unlikely places. He said that he would prefer to hire a poor kid from the Irish Channel area of New Orleans rather than a silver spoon Harvard grad if the inner city kid had heart. "Be back here Wednesday morning at nine o'clock," Mr. Nick said.

He realized Desmond owned only one suit, a fact that was evident after multiple meetings. On Wednesday morning he took Desmond shopping. Mr. Nick invested five thousand dollars of his own money in business suits, ties, and shoes for Desmond. Wearing new clothes gave Desmond remarkable confidence. "Nice clothes make you feel better than having a wallet full of cash," Mr. Nick said. He was right. Desmond learned how to tie a necktie correctly and polish real leather shoes. "Throughout the day check your appearance. Make sure your tie is straight, shirt tucked in tight, belt buckle lined up! To be successful, you must look successful," Mr. Brandages advised.

Desmond was given eight weeks to prepare for the Series 7 exam. This was the general securities license required by the

National Association of Securities Dealers (NASD) for anyone wishing to work as a stockbroker. The firm gave Desmond a stack of books, placed him in an empty cubicle, and told him to "study." The material was easy to understand because it was similar to the subjects Desmond had covered while studying economics at Tulane: international markets, options, derivatives, and municipal bonds. However, Waterman provided no assistance other than the collection of books; it was professional Darwinism, survival of the most determined. Desmond studied all day long, every day. He ate lunch at his desk to save time.

John was a Waterman trainee hired two weeks earlier. He was confident since his Series 7 practice test scores were in the eighties, well above the minimum passing grade of seventy. But he scored a failing sixty-eight, did not return to the office, and his name was never mentioned again. "John was confident yet he failed. Yes, I am nervous!" Desmond confessed to Mr. Nick.

"I did not fire John, he fired himself! Forget about John! What happened to him has no impact on your career with Waterman. It's like flipping a coin. The result of one flip does not affect the next. It's always fifty-fifty odds. Focus and pass your exams as expected," Mr. Brandages said.

The Series 7 was administered at a downtown New Orleans hotel. Desmond walked upstairs to the third floor, down a long hall, and turned right. The exam room was furnished with sixty individual desks spaced evenly apart. Proctors were dressed in white shirts, black ties, and black pants. The clock counted down the seconds to either the start of a lucrative career or humiliation and failure. Desmond was distracted by the constant back-and-forth marching of the proctors, each patrolling an assigned area of the exam room. They seemed to approach quietly from the back, sneaking up upon anyone desperate enough or unprepared enough to attempt cheating. Desmond finished before time was up. He turned in his test booklet at the front desk, returned the pencils, and walked across Canal Street to the soda fountain in the Kress Department Store. Desmond enjoyed a hamburger and crème soda, confident he had done well.

The next week went by slowly as Desmond waited for the test results. He tried studying for the Series 63. The 63 exam allowed brokers to be licensed in states other than their state of domicile. It was much easier than the Series 7, but concentration was difficult. Desmond began looking back over the Series 7 study material and second-guessing his answers. "Mr. Desmond Dupree, please report to the manager's office," Mr. Brandages' assistant announced over the office PA system. The short walk from his cubicle to Mr. Nick's office seemed difficult, a forced march leading to a very unpleasant fate. Desmond sat in a leather chair at a round table with his hands clenched tightly into nervous fists. His stomach was beginning to turn, and breathing became difficult.

Mr. Brandages sat across from him and opened an envelope; he read the results. "You passed with a score of ninety-four. Congratulations." He shook Desmond's hand as he got up from the table.

Desmond looked surprised. "Is that it?"

"Why, are you expecting special accolades for doing what I hired you to do?" Mr. Brandages replied.

Desmond completed the additional tests. These were nothing compared to the difficulty of the Series 7 exam, and failure resulted in an embarrassing retake, not termination.

2

DESMOND WAS NERVOUS ABOUT THE New York flight. "Mr. Brandages, do you mind if I take the train back?" he asked. "I leave New York on Friday, and I don't need to be back here until Monday." Mr. Brandages was always looking for ways to cut expenses, and the train would save a few dollars. Desmond booked a reservation at the New Orleans Amtrak Union Passenger Terminal. "How will you pay for this, young man?" the ticket clerk asked.

"Just charge it to Waterman Securities. I have a card number," Desmond replied proudly. A one-way airline ticket for the flight to New York was purchased automatically through Waterman's travel department in Desmond's name, as was common practice.

Desmond loved trains and looked forward to a relaxing ride home. It would allow two full days to collect his thoughts, review the training material, and prepare for his first day back as a real investment banker. Desmond's grandfather was a conductor on the old L&N railroad. He often invited young Desmond to spend summer evenings sitting in the engineer's seat as the locomotives moved cars around the New Orleans rail yard. "I wasn't given an Amtrak receipt; they said everything has been taken care of," Desmond explained to Mr. Brandages' secretary.

"That doesn't seem right somehow, but no one takes trains anymore! You are the first in many years," she said.

Desmond looked forward to the long train ride home but was anxious about the flight to New York. He had to make a connection in Atlanta, then on to Newark. He had no idea how to find his way around the Atlanta and Newark airports, check baggage, or find his gate. "Desmond, here are instructions to help you find your way. Look at the airport monitors to check your flight and gate assignment. Keep your boarding passes separate. Place your luggage claim ticket in your wallet. When you arrive in Newark, someone will be waiting for you at the gate. They will hold up your name on a card." Mr. Brandages had carefully written everything down along with his home phone numbers. "Don't worry, you will be fine," he assured Desmond.

Desmond followed the directions and arrived at the Newark airport without much trouble. A short man in a black suit was waiting at the gate holding a small sign with Desmond's name. "Welcome to New York," the driver said as he picked up Desmond's luggage. They walked together to a Chrysler airport limo parked outside the main entrance. The driver was talkative and asked many questions.

The Waterman training campus and corporate headquarters were located in Princeton, New Jersey, near the university. Most training class work was offered in the conference center. Restaurants and Waterman's own hotel and bar were nearby. Trainees also worked in New York City and on the floor of the New York Stock Exchange as part of the program.

A doorman dressed somewhat like a British soldier from colonial India opened the limo door. He collected Desmond's suitcase and directed him to the registration desk. "This way, sir." Desmond never knew such a place could exist—curving staircase, marble floors, walls of windows overlooking manicured grounds.

"Can I help you, sir?" a beautiful Princeton undergrad asked from behind the registration desk.

"Desmond Dupree, here for Training Class Three-Thirteen," he said confidently. Desmond's room was down the hall on the third floor. The restaurant was on the first floor with a nearby bar. "There are no charges or tabs for anything. Enjoy your stay and good luck," she said.

Desmond's class was the first group to use the new Princeton facility. All previous WS training was done in New York City. Workers were still doing last-minute adjustments as the eager members of Training Class 313 arrived. Desmond found the restaurant and ordered a hamburger, eating alone at a table for four. He enjoyed eating alone in crowded restaurants, watching others, wondering about their lives and relationships, finding the solitude comforting.

Desmond had noticed that eating alone for some people was painful; they hid behind books or newspapers, repeatedly looking at their watch as if disappointed that expected friends had not arrived, fooling no one. The psychological pre-hire profiles Desmond completed for Waterman Securities asked many questions about solitude. The responses indicated something, but what, exactly, remained a mystery.

When Desmond approached his room, a construction worker emerged, explaining something about "trouble-shooting" electrical issues. Desmond didn't pay much attention and was eager to get a decent night's rest and start fresh tomorrow. The electrical problems were related to the in-room fire alarm system. A flashing red light and siren activated every twenty minutes, all night long. Desmond called the front desk at 2:00 a.m. "Please, do something, the fire alarm goes off every few minutes, and I can't sleep!" he said. The clerk explained that it was a new building and they were working to correct the problems.

"Please remember any attempt to disable the alarm is a federal offense and a violation of WS policy!" the clerk said.

Desmond arrived at the New Jersey Transit station platform at 5:30 a.m., planning to be on Wall Street by 7:00 a.m. The other Waterman trainees all looked tired, with bloodshot eyes and dark circles. "What the hell is wrong with those fire alarms? I'm sleeping in the lobby tonight!" another trainee said. The fresh suits and new briefcases told everyone they were rookies.

New Jersey Transit operated slow-moving commuter trains into Manhattan's Penn Station, stopping at each city along the way like city buses. Amtrak commuter trains shared some of the same tracks. Although tired, Desmond stood first in line on the platform with Dave, a Waterman trainee from Nebraska.

A train could be seen approaching in the distance. "I wouldn't stand in front of that yellow line if I were you!" a local said, while pointing toward the thick line painted across the width of the platform about five feet from the edge. Amtrak operated high-speed electric commuters between major East Coast cities. They traveled at nearly eighty miles per hour and kept tight schedules. Desmond and Dave looked down at the yellow warning line, unaware of its significance. The approaching train was Amtrak, not the slow New Jersey Transit. They were standing near the platform edge as the speeding train, with horns blaring, passed within a few feet. "What the hell type of train is that?" Desmond wondered.

"Nothing like that in Nebraska!" Dave said.

The local commuter shook his head in a display of perceived superiority. "I told you! Pay attention to the yellow lines. They are there for a reason," he said sarcastically.

The New Jersey Transit train crept along the tracks like a snail but eventually reached the Princeton station. The seat backs could slide over, depending on which way the train was heading, similar to New Orleans streetcars familiar to Desmond. There was standing room only. Many riders held on to straps attached to the ceiling while reading the paper and drinking coffee at the same time. Conductors walked between the cars punching tickets. Dave and Desmond were standing among the crowd. A conductor with a heavy New York accent announced the name of each town as the train rolled along. "Did he say New York?" Desmond asked Dave.

"Yes, I think so," Dave said. They picked up their empty new briefcases and eagerly waited for their stop. The car slowed down, doors opened, and they exited quickly as the train moved on.

There was trash and broken wine and beer bottles everywhere. Homeless people were sleeping on benches, covered with newspaper. The walls, floors, and ceilings were spray-painted with threatening gang tags. The nearby buildings were burned out, and the entire place smelled like urine. "My god! This place looks like Beirut." Desmond looked around. "The conductor didn't say N-E-W Y-O-R-K, he said N-E-W-A-R-K. We're in downtown Newark!" Desmond said. The next Transit train was due in twenty minutes. Desmond and Dave sat on a bench back to back so no one could sneak up on them.

They reached New York and Penn Station nearly an hour behind schedule. Waterman Securities provided walking directions, but they only had fifteen minutes before classes started. "How fast can you get us to the Waterman building near the Financial District?" Desmond asked a cab driver.

"No worries. Get in," the cabbie said.

The driver ignored red lights and stop signs. Desmond and Dave held on as the Crown Victoria sped toward the Waterman Building. At the approaching red light, another car had already stopped. The cab driver jumped the curb and drove on the sidewalk with windows down, yelling and screaming and waving his arms, horn blowing. "Out of the way, out of the way!" A pedestrian ducked into a doorway but dropped his briefcase. The cab's wheels crushed it. "I warned you! Out of the way! Your fault!" The driver gave him the finger. Desmond looked back. The man was angry but unharmed.

"I got your medallion number. You bastard, I got your number!" the man was screaming back at the taxi while trying to pick up his papers.

3

EVERY LISTED STOCK TRADES AT its own post on the floor of the New York Stock Exchange. A specialist manages price movements to make sure the market remains orderly. The bid price is what buyers are willing to pay. The ask price is what sellers are willing to accept. The difference between each is the "spread." On busy news days, overwhelming sell or buy orders can create price imbalances that specialists smooth out, using their own money to create market stability. Specialists take huge risks and can make and lose fortunes in a single day. They also receive one-eighth of a point override on every share traded.

Desmond was assigned to work with the specialist at the HADA-COL Cosmetics "symbol HC" post. "You nickel dicks come around every few months. Stay out of my way and try not to fuck anything up!" the specialist told Desmond.

Being on the floor of the Stock Exchange was an incredible experience. For the first few days Desmond sat and watched, doing nothing important. He delivered messages, picked up lunch, and stayed out of the way, as instructed. It was enough just to be there.

"If you could do anything at all, what would that be?" the specialist asked during an unusually quiet time. "I'm not talking about bullshit like buying a boat or something. Anyone can do that. What would you do if there were absolutely no limits on what you could pick?" Desmond had never thought about that. "Would you want to cross the Rubicon with Caesar's Legions? Would you want to spend the winter at Valley Forge with George Washington? Would you want to sit atop an Apollo rocket during the final ten-second countdown before a moon shot? Think about it, Nickel Dick." The specialist was distracted momentarily as a trader asked to see the order book status. "To be an American capitalist is the correct answer." The specialist looked back in Desmond's direction. "A thousand years from now, historians will be envious of us. Never in the history of mankind has any single nation's economic hegemony been so complete. Fuck Caesar!" he said. "We're American capitalists! Masters of our universe! Strap yourself in and hold on. You are about to get educated," the specialist said. "There is a rumor on the street, HADACOL Cosmetics is the target of a hostile takeover!"

Usually the HC post was relatively quiet, but that was changing. A group of traders in red, yellow, and blue jackets surrounded the post. Each jacket color represented different trading organizations. All were trying to buy HADACOL stock at the same time. The fast market went from $6.35 per share to $8.15 in a matter of minutes. "I need fifteen hundred at $8.15, do $8.20!" Many traders were shouting and waving their arms.

Everyone was yelling at once and sending hand signals to other traders and their associates standing to the side of the post, away from the action, recording trade confirmations. The specialist frantically worked his book, selling and buying, trying to manage the spread in a reasonable fashion. He yelled the fast-moving quotes back to Desmond, who entered the escalating prices on the Quotron machine for broadcast to eager brokers around the country. "Stay with me, Nickel Dick, don't fuck up," he said without looking in Desmond's direction. "Do not fuck this up!"

When the closing bell finally rang at 4:00 p.m., Desmond was exhausted. "Why are you tired? We live for days like this. Get excited, Nickel Dick," the specialist said with a trembling voice, overcome with adrenaline. "How many minutes were erased from the Watergate tapes?" he asked Desmond.

"What?" Desmond responded, surprised by the unusual question.

"You heard me. Answer the damn question," the specialist demanded.

Desmond thought for a moment and said, "Eighteen and a half."

"That's right." He handed Desmond ten one-hundred-dollar bills. "Forget about derivatives, calculus, and B-school bullshit. Information is the only thing of any real value in this business. You just earned one thousand bucks because you had specific knowledge. That is the real lesson; never forget the importance of information." He held out his hand. "We haven't been properly introduced. The name is Rob. You did real good!"

4

THE WEEKENDS WERE FREE TIME, so Dave and Desmond decided to visit Manhattan like tourists. Dave made reservations at the Milford Plaza hotel for about 120 dollars a night, very expensive by the standards of New Orleans or the Midwest, but not much at all for New York City. The New Jersey Transit reached Penn Station on time; a line of cabs were waiting outside at the side entrance. The first cab in line approached as Desmond raised his hand. "Taxi!" Desmond felt he was beginning to learn the New York ropes. "Milford Plaza, please," he said.

The driver opened the trunk, tossed their small bags in, and slid behind the wheel. "The Milford Plaza, right?" he repeated. The ride was longer than expected, but they got to see much of the city and enjoyed the driver's commentary. It was unbelievable how quickly the fare added up. Even as they sat at red lights, the meter rolled. After about thirty-five minutes they reached the hotel and split the forty-five-dollar charge plus five-dollar tip.

"We appreciate the ride. Thanks for getting us here quickly," Dave said.

"We love tourists. Thank you," the driver said as he drove off.

The Milford was a dump, having been a former welfare hotel and only recently somewhat converted to private commercial use. It reminded Desmond of hotels on Airline Highway in New Orleans that rented rooms by the hour, except the Milford was thirty-five stories tall. Their room was on the fifteenth floor. As the elevator doors opened, Desmond and Dave stepped over a drunk sleeping on the floor and walked to their room at the end of a long hall. Desmond threw his bag on the bed, brushed his teeth, and decided to explore New York on foot. Dave wanted to stay in the room and rest.

Desmond walked about a block, looked to his left, and saw Penn Station. "Excuse me! How many Penn Stations are there in New York?" he asked a police officer, who answered with a puzzled look.

"Only one Penn Station. Are you on drugs?"

Desmond explained the unnecessarily long taxi ride and asked about any possible recourse. "That's too bad! Next time don't be so stupid!" the policeman said.

Too aggravated to finish his walk, Desmond went back to the Milford, but could not open the room door. "Dave, wake up. I can't open the door!" Dave was afraid someone would kick their way into the room, so he had blocked the door with a heavy dresser.

Taking the subway seemed easy enough, except that some stations had various levels of tracks and trains running in many different directions from the same location. It was all very confusing because there were no easily visible landmarks underground. Desmond and Dave intended to reach Times Square but never found the correct stop. "We have been riding a long time. Maybe we should see where we are." They emerged from the subterranean maze in a residential area on a street lined with neat brick homes built right up to the sidewalk. At the center of the block was a large Catholic church. Each end of the street was barricaded and manned by two NYPD officers. It was the annual parish fair. "You are welcome to attend, but we won't tolerate trouble," the officer said as he opened the barricade enough for Desmond and Dave to walk by.

The locals treated Desmond and Dave like family. They were offered Polish sausage sandwiches and cold beer and were announced as visiting guests. Extra chairs were brought over from a nearby home.

They shared a table with a proud family who had produced four generations of New York City firemen. Their oldest daughter, Grace, was now a senior at City University.

The band played Sinatra hits, and raffle winners were announced between songs. The highlight of the evening was the crowning of the fair's queen. Grace won. Desmond admired her beauty. She walked off the stage and reached for his hand. They danced again and again. Grace reminded Desmond of pleasant things he loved, like coffee in the afternoon. Later they planned to sneak off together, walking along a path toward a neighborhood park.

Grace and Desmond held hands. She stopped and turned to him as the moon's light penetrated the mist. Bordering the park were federal-type buildings, a fountain, and benches. In the middle of the square stood a single live oak with muscular branches that reached skyward, then arched back to the ground, a sensible compromise negotiated with gravity's relentless tug. The oak stood strong, determined and inviting, nonjudgmental. Sheltered under the oak's embrace, Desmond and Grace stayed the night, talking like reunited family, watching the night drift by and loving each other.

Desmond picked up an acorn and put it in his pocket, swapping it for the love he would leave behind. He planted the acorn in his front yard at home. Each day Desmond greeted the growing oak like an old friend. He did not harbor sentimental delusions about returning again. He knew Grace would move on with her life. It was enough to know the oak would endure.

Desmond and Grace did promise to remember that night forever. When things turned difficult, Desmond treasured those happy memories. They provided comfort and shelter from life's storms. He often wondered what became of Grace and whether she kept her promise and remembered him. Desmond wondered what mattered, if anything did. It meant nothing to him if he was freezing in cold rain at a bus stop or eating lunch alone in a crowded restaurant. His mind could be someplace else, somewhere better, always dancing with Grace.

The second week of Waterman's training program involved acquiring extensive product knowledge. Desmond aced this. He loved learning about puts and calls, margin, bonds and equities. This was relatively easy for him, while others struggled, but the amount of time spent learning real estate issues surprised him. The class studied subprime mortgage loans and collateralization. They learned that groups of high-risk mortgage loans could be combined, creating an investment rated AAA and sold to investors. Waterman had recently started a new real estate division. Mortgages would become an important part of the company's business plan.

Desmond was asked by another trainee to help her prepare for the final exams. They met in the Waterman lounge and studied for hours. Conversation eventually became personal. She was from California and had a successful career in real estate. She opened her purse. "These are my children," she remarked as she showed Desmond photos of three beautiful children, all less than ten years old. "This is my husband; we married twelve years ago." He was handsome, and they appeared to be the perfect family. Desmond reluctantly surrendered any thought of sleeping with her.

She stared at her husband's picture and held it tightly in her hands. "Just before I left for training, he confessed that he's in love with someone else. He wants a divorce," she said. Desmond did not know what to say. She was crying now. "I need to feel wanted. Please stay with me tonight," she asked Desmond. Her pain was so deep he could physically sense it. He felt it in his stomach. He felt it in his heart. He was overcome by her sadness. He did not understand those feelings; they were not sexual. Desmond reached out to her. She placed her head on his shoulder and cried.

5

THE TRAINING CLASS WAS RANDOMLY divided into two separate groups, A and B. Each group was led to a room with telephones lining the walls. "This is the sales component of training. We will make sales calls to each other. Waterman personnel will listen in and score individual sales performance," the lead trainer said. "On Friday, we make live cold calls to real prospects in your hometowns."

Mr. Brandages prepared Desmond for this, and he had a script ready. "This is Desmond Dupree with Waterman Securities. I am working to build my business. Do you currently have anyone handling your investments?" Desmond would then be quiet and let the prospect answer. "I am sure you are in good hands, but may I send you my card? If ever you want a second opinion, I would appreciate the opportunity to earn your business." Desmond always went for the appointment and would ask prospective clients to meet at his office. If they drove to the Waterman office, then he was sure he could open the account and earn their business.

During the first midmorning break Dave met Desmond in the hallway between the two classrooms. "Did you know this was a sales job? I thought we were managing money for wealthy individuals!" Dave was deeply upset. "Where did you think the accounts came from?" Desmond asked him. "They don't just fall from the sky."

After the break Dave was not in class. He resigned and caught the first flight home to Nebraska. Desmond would never see or hear from Dave again.

Training ended. Everyone said their good-byes and received a certificate during a dinner ceremony. Waterman personnel were all on stage, including a short man in a black suit. Desmond recognized him as the airport limo driver! Was the fire alarm problem part of a setup as well? Desmond wondered. The Waterman CEO was scheduled to attend the ceremony and share words of encouragement. With no official seating assignments, many class members arrived hours early, trying to score one of the coveted spots at the first table. The CEO most likely hated dinner with trainees, considering them a time-consuming nuisance. Nothing good could come of this.

Desmond selected a seat at a back table, as far away as possible from the CEO. He quietly enjoyed dinner and was careful not to draw attention to himself. While seated with the CEO, a stupid trainee told numerous off-color homosexual jokes that he thought were outrageously funny. Others at the table laughed. The CEO showed no reaction. After dinner, WS security personnel were waiting for those involved. They were fired, escorted off the property, and driven to the airport. Their careers over before they started.

Desmond headed to the Amtrak station. He had the shuttle bus to himself since his classmates all went to airports. "Desmond Dupree, Mr. Desmond Dupree." A porter in a starched white uniform was standing on the platform calling his name.

"I'm Desmond, is there a problem?" a confused Desmond asked.

"This way, sir." Desmond was escorted to a private sleeping car and shown his exclusive room, like a first-class cabin on the *Orient Express*. "Do you like to read the papers? May I have your shoes? I will bring the dinner menu momentarily. Have I missed anything?" the porter inquired.

At each city the porter got a newspaper and brought it to Desmond. His shined shoes were placed in a small compartment in time for dinner. Only one other passenger was traveling in similar style, the Amtrak chief financial officer. The other passengers were not allowed to enter the dining car until Desmond and the Amtrak officer had finished their meal. "What do you do for Waterman? Usually passengers in these cars are much older," the CFO asked.

After dinner, Desmond's full-size bed was turned down and chocolate candy placed on his pillows. He arrived back in New Orleans Sunday evening and reported to work Monday morning.

"Mr. Dupree, please report to the manager's office." Desmond assumed he would be congratulated for outstanding efforts and successful completion of the training program. He was wrong.

"Give me one good reason why I should not fire you right now!" Mr. Brandages asked angrily. "Do you realize how deeply you have embarrassed me?"

Confused, Desmond had no idea what he had done wrong. Mr. Brandages slammed a three-page invoice on the table. "Spending twenty-two hundred dollars on a one-way train ride was absurd. Fifty dollars for shoe shines! Twenty-five dollars for newspapers! Five hundred dollars for meals! You travel like the Czar of Russia? Are you out of your mind?" Mr. Brandages asked angrily. His face was red and his hands shook as he waved the invoice. Desmond tried to explain. Mr. Brandages read a new nationwide travel policy for Waterman personnel in all branches. "From this date forward, no WS employees are allowed to utilize Amtrak trains for company business travel. No exceptions." Mr. Brandages said he had never heard of a trainee impacting company procedures in such a dramatic way. The "Dupree Policy" remained in place, Desmond's legacy.

6

THE BEST WAY TO KEEP his job was to work harder and smarter than anyone else. Desmond purchased a list of successful small-business owners in New Orleans. Every cold call was worthwhile because each name on the list was a qualified investor. He developed a point system to track his cold-calling progress, awarding points for various business-building activities. Maintaining a high activity level would help sustain confidence until he opened new accounts. Unlike experienced brokers, Desmond would not have client appointments lined up throughout the day, so he earned a sense of achievement by reaching two hundred daily points on his activity sheet.

Talking to an eligible investor was worth one point. Setting an appointment was worth two points. Having an appointment was good for five points, and opening an account was ten points. Receiving a referral was also ten points. He did not award any points for commission earnings because he did not want the temptation to take the rest of the day off. People did not like receiving cold calls, especially busy entrepreneurs. "I'm trying to build my business, just like you! You don't like receiving these calls; try making two hundred every day!" Desmond always got the appointment.

Although Desmond had his own list of prospects, he still had to complete the daily call cards provided by Mr. Brandages. He dialed the first number. A woman answered the phone. "May I speak to Dr.

Thomas?" Desmond asked. The woman assumed he was a patient and woke the doctor. "This is Desmond Dupree with Waterman Securities. Do you currently have anyone handling your investments?"

The doctor became angry. "Young man, I have been on call for sixteen hours. Never dial this number again! Do you understand?" Desmond apologized after the doctor threatened to file a complaint with the office manager. "I'm going back to sleep. Never call this number again!" he repeated.

Ralph sat in the adjacent cubicle. He was also a trainee and a practical jokester. Desmond thought it would be fun to turn the tables. "Hey, Ralph, I can't finish all my calls today. Can you help me out, old buddy?" Desmond asked as he reached over and handed Ralph a stack of contact cards, placing the Dr. Thomas card on top.

"Dr. Thomas, this is Ralph Mills with Waterman Securities. Do you need insured, tax-free income?" Ralph held the phone far from his ear with a surprised look. Desmond could hear the doctor demanding to speak to the office manager immediately. "You bastard! I will get you!" Ralph said, placing the phone down. "He is calling Brandages now! Holy shit! We're screwed."

"Desmond Dupree and Ralph Mills, report to the manager's office," Mr. Brandages' assistant announced over the office intercom system. First thing next morning, the doctor, true to his word, was waiting in Mr. Brandages' office. "I will not tolerate unprofessional behavior. I promise you, Dr. Thomas, I will get to the bottom of this," Mr. Brandages said. After a half-hour discussion, the meeting ended and the doctor left satisfied. The matter was settled. Desmond and Ralph quietly awaited their punishment like disobedient children.

"He is a fire starter!" Mr. Brandages said in a friendly tone after the doctor left, someone spreading problems unnecessarily. "Ralph, get back to work and finish your calls. Desmond, stay for a minute." Ralph was happy to leave. "Learn to channel your remarkable ability.

I've never hired anyone more talented or more difficult to manage than you," Mr. Brandages said to Desmond.

The day was long, but Desmond still did not have two hundred points. The next name on his call list was the owner of an all-you-can-eat fried mullet restaurant. He was tempted to skip it and move on to a more promising name, but Desmond had learned that success was often found in unlikely places. "Mr. Brill, this is Desmond Dupree with Waterman Securities. Do you currently have anyone handling your investments?" Mr. Brill was polite and soon began to ask questions about individual stock picks and natural gas futures. *Natural gas! What is his interest in natural gas?* Desmond wondered.

Mr. Brill was president of the board for a large utility company. The mullet restaurant was his family's business. He opened an account with Desmond and did well investing in liquefied natural gas and writing covered calls. Mr. Brill understood these markets since power plants are natural-gas fired. He continued to add additional funds and open other accounts. He referred family, friends, and associates. Soon Desmond had accounts for most board members, the company 401(k), and when the CEO retired, Desmond got that account too. Louisiana's largest power plant was named after Desmond's client. One cold call to a mullet restaurant owner had made Desmond's career. He'd almost skipped to a "more promising name" further down the list. *Funny how life works,* he thought.

The Waterman office on Poydras and St. Charles Avenue had a bullpen at its center that sat nearly fifty new trainees in small cubicles. Individual Quotron machines sat on lazy Susans, each rotating between two desks. Every broker had at least one phone with a rotary dial and five buttons across the bottom lighting up, indicating incoming calls.

Successful brokers sat in glass offices along the outside walls with two or three phones on their desks. Stock orders were written on paper tickets and sent to the wire room using vacuum tubes. The wire room had more employees than the office had brokers, each sitting at a teletype, sending orders to the New York exchange floor. If tickets were entered in the morning, confirmations would arrive before market close. Brokers kept track of client activity in black books and entered daily trades by hand.

Across the back wall was a large tickertape display showing current trade quotes across a screen using small colored lights, green representing an uptick in price, red a downtick trade. Rows of theater-type chairs were arranged in the lobby with a view of the tickertape display. Wealthy investors rode the streetcar line from the University area and smoked cigars while dressed in seersucker suits. They sat in the theater chairs, watching stock prices and constantly making calculations in small notebooks. Success for young brokers could be assured by landing some of these lucrative trading accounts. Desmond had a few. "Desmond, buy two hundred Ford, at market now!" The order was yelled from the chairs, and a hand was raised holding a lit cigar.

Desmond placed the trade and earned a two-hundred-dollar commission. "Yes sir, Mr. Dunbar, anything else?" This went on all day long, with Desmond earning a commission on each buy or sell.

On a mid-October Friday the market began trading out of range and lost about one hundred points, a particularly large decline by the standards of the day. Desmond called his clients. "On Monday morning we should place sell orders," he advised. "It won't hurt to protect recent profits." He had over twenty sell orders ready for Monday's open.

Desmond parked in a lot near the river, walked down Poydras Street, picked up the *Wall Street Journal,* and stopped at Mother's restaurant for a remnant ham biscuit. Remnants were pieces of leftover ham from the bottom of the pan that had time to absorb the sweet juices. The pieces were piled high on homemade biscuits. This was Desmond's favorite time of day, especially with a cup of café au lait. He took a few minutes to eat breakfast and read the *Journal.*

Desmond sat at his desk and wrote twenty sell tickets. He carefully reviewed each one individually, walked over to the vacuum tube, and sent the orders. Each morning at 7:00 central time, Waterman Securities hosted a nationwide market update call over the "squawk box" system. Desmond pulled up a chair and listened. Participating in the morning call was a job requirement, but Desmond viewed it as a waste of time. Usually, it was an effort by Waterman's trading desks to liquidate unprofitable positions held in house accounts. The call offered enhanced commission payout to brokers willing to convince clients to buy these disappointing investments. Desmond wanted no part of that.

This call was different from the start, with a real sense of urgency. Waterman traders and economists discussed an overwhelming sell imbalance in the futures market. They were scared! Not Desmond. He felt relaxed, as he already had sell orders in place. His trade executions would be first in line when the market opened. Desmond sat at his desk and waited for the 8:30 opening bell, confident that his clients were protected.

The Quotron machine listed each stock symbol, followed by a line of dots until trading started. Once trading began, the dots were replaced by live price quotes. The markets opened on time, but no prices were displayed. Desmond slapped the side of the Quotron machine but still only dots. Twenty minutes later, still only dots. The problem wasn't with the Quotron. "My god, my god!" Desmond shouted. "It's the floor specialists; they can't balance the bids and asks! They can't find a balance!"

Sporadically prices begin to appear, down unbelievable amounts: GM down 3.75, CAT down 4.25, JNJ down 2.35, over twenty percent on the averages. Desmond called the wire room to make sure his sell orders were entered. "All lines are tied up. Nothing can get to the exchange. The system is overwhelmed. Sorry, Desmond, doing what we can." Then client calls began, all phone lines lit up, and the lobby filled with desperate investors, reporters, and the curious.

"Sell, sell everything. Sell at market, get whatever you can!" Traders panicked as falling prices moved across the ticker.

Around lunchtime a man walked into the office dressed like a housepainter. He wore white overalls, splattered with many different paint colors. He had paint under his fingernails, wore a white hat, and held a Sony Walkman, listening to a James Taylor cassette tape. Desmond was near the lobby. "I'm Desmond Dupree. May I help you?" The man asked if he could have a minute to discuss stock investments. They walked over to Desmond's cubicle and sat down.

"I would like to get one hundred shares of IBM," he said.

Desmond was surprised because no one was buying anything. "You want to buy?" he asked. Signs of a deepening market panic spreading across the country were hard to ignore, and selling was rampant. "Watching the news, I realized that never again in my lifetime would I be able to buy IBM at these low prices," the painter said.

On this day markets lost nearly twenty-five percent of total value. However, most of these losses were recovered within the next few weeks. Those investors who did not panic eventually did well; others who made emotional decisions suffered long-term losses and never recovered. Experts were selling everything, ignoring strong macro fundamentals. The smartest man around on this day was a house-painter buying one hundred IBM shares at the market. But he was wrong. It was not the lowest market he would ever see. For Desmond, October 19th was the learning opportunity of a lifetime.

7

OFFICE SALES MEETINGS WERE HELD about every six months in the meeting room of the Interuniversal Hotel adjacent to the Waterman office. Everyone walked over together through the corridor connecting the two buildings. It looked like a convention of dark suits. Mr. Brandages addressed the meeting. "Working for Waterman Securities is like playing for the Yankees. We expect to win, always! We have hired some great new people, and I am excited about our future." He walked over from the podium and locked the door. Anyone not in the room was locked out. "Being late is a career decision," according to Mr. Brandages. "We have great opportunity here. I have an investment idea that I expect each of you to embrace with your best efforts." Mr. Brandages described a small southern manufacturing company specializing in flatbed trailer trucks. Desmond had seen the name on the backs of trailers for years: Daresay.

"Daresay is expanding their product line. The new product will soon be in every American home. It is a ground-floor opportunity. It will be everywhere in six months!" Mr. Brandages said excitedly. "Daresay already has contracts in hand with major consumer products companies! Best of all, the stock price has not yet reacted. At five dollars it is trading at six-month lows!"

Desmond knew that fooling the market was nearly impossible. Usually a stock price reflects economic equilibrium, seldom overlooking value. Markets are comprised of intelligent people researching every angle of a company's prospects. The price is the average of what investors think a stock is worth. If markets priced a stock at the low end of its range, Desmond did not question that assessment, nor would he question Mr. Brandages.

"I have with me today a sample of this revolutionary product. One of the first available." Mr. Brandages reached down for a small container and removed the item. He placed it on the podium for everyone to see.

"Is it made of plastic? What is it? That's amazing!" The room was abuzz waiting for Mr. Brandages to explain.

"This is the world's very first plastic soft drink can." It had a plastic body, but the top and pull tab were aluminum. "It has many advantages over regular cans, including durability and low cost," Mr. Brandages said. The plastic can was passed around for everyone to see. Another broker quietly said the plastic can was "like a Galapagos finch, bound for extinction." Mr. Brandages answered questions, then dismissed everyone to "hit" the phones. Daresay's stock price began to move up as predicted.

Mr. Brandages always had change in his pockets; he jingled it as he walked around the office. Usually he could be heard approaching, giving everyone time to look busy. Desmond was concentrating on the Quotron machine, studying news on Daresay. He did not hear Mr. Brandages approach. Desmond turned and saw Mr. Brandages standing by his desk. "Desmond Dupree, I did not hire you to be an analyst! Pick up that phone and sell something!" Desmond wondered who would need or want a plastic can anyway. They already had plastic bottles, and the regular cans seemed to do just fine. But for the next week Daresay stock was up every day. Desmond called some clients and purchased a few hundred shares.

He noticed that the stock price was moving up, but the daily volume was light. The only people buying the stock were the New Orleans office of WS. Desmond sold his clients' shares for a nice profit. The Exchange newspaper picked up on the plastic can story and the unusual stock price movement. They wrote an investigative article. Daresay did not have any contracts, as stated by Mr. Brandages, only letters of intent. Upon further research, it was determined it cost more than three times the price of a regular can to manufacture a plastic can. Within a few days the stock price was down seventy percent. Coke announced it had no interest in plastic cans. Desmond did not feel right about this deal from the beginning, but had felt pressured to participate. He learned to always trust his instincts, to always go with his gut feeling.

In the competitive Waterman world, nothing was guaranteed, especially job security. New hires were compared against all other members of their national training class on a quarterly basis. Branch managers received performance reports comparing net new assets, revenues, and total assets under management. Trainees were divided into quintiles based on a formula measuring these categories. There were no variables in the method controlling for city size or inherited assets. Some new hires inherited business or joined successful teams, creating a distinct advantage. Still, Mr. Brandages fired anyone in the bottom quintile. "I have no tolerance for losers. I will show you how to be successful, if you have the right attitude. If not, pack your stuff and leave," he said.

The glass private offices along the exterior walls were up for grabs on a quarterly basis. Hotshot new brokers always had a chance to unseat a veteran under the right circumstances, causing disgrace and humiliation for the loser moving down to a cubicle in the bullpen. It was like the old west. As soon as someone became the fastest gun, there was always another ready to challenge.

Mr. John had been with the company for thirty-five years, starting after a failed attempt at commercial banking. For a number of years he was a leading producer and earned the managing director title, a prestigious honor. Desmond walked into the restroom one morning and saw Mr. John combing black dye into his hair, trying to hide the gray. Desmond hoped he, himself, would be traveling and enjoying life at an advanced age. He did not want to end up still pitching at seventy. Lately Mr. John's health was failing, and many of his clients were dying off. Mr. Brandages called him in after the market closed.

"We have two spots open in the bullpen. I will allow you to pick the one you want," he said.

When Mr. John arrived for work the next day, a young broker was already looking over the office. He was measuring the walls with a tape measure. "I want to move in tomorrow morning. Have all your crap out today," he said.

Mr. John called a few clients but knew his revenue numbers would never measure up. He sat and stared out the window, watching business people hurrying about the city. He turned around, placed his head in his hands, and wondered how he would pay mounting medical expenses. Mr. John died at his desk, a victim of an intentional prescription medication overdose. No one realized he was dead; most assumed he was resting. It was the night cleaning crew who called 911.

Desmond did not need to worry about job security. He was in the top quintile, still earning two hundred points each day for prospecting. Most of his points were now from appointments and new accounts, although he still set two hours each day for prospecting new business. Desmond was a real "cold-calling cowboy." The Waterman Forbs Award was given for reaching 280,000 dollars in revenue during the first eighteen months of production, as a new hire. In Waterman's history only sixty-eight brokers had reached this level. Desmond Dupree was the first winner from New Orleans. Mr. Brandages received an 8,500-dollar bonus for his role in Desmond's success. He gave the money to Desmond.

A trip to Hawaii was included with the award. The Waterman Forbs winners and other top brokers were invited on the recognition trip in mid-December. They flew a Boeing jet from New Orleans to Houston, then nonstop to Honolulu. After a short layover, they flew Hawaiian Air to the small airport on the island of Kauai, the least developed island but the most beautiful. It was also the poorest island, with almost no industry and only two major resorts. Local government limited the height of buildings to that of the tallest palm trees. Desmond invited his friend Karen to join him. They had become close and always enjoyed each other's company. When Desmond went to New York, Karen joined the Navy Reserves and was currently stationed at the Great Lakes Naval Air Station north of Chicago. She was happy to escape the Chicago winter and arranged for leave to correspond with Desmond's Hawaiian trip. He planned to propose to her during the trip.

Karen and Desmond stayed at the island's best resort and planned a boat trip to see the Napoli cliffs. After a short bus ride to a small oceanside harbor, they boarded a rubber Zodiac boat. Three Hawaiians sat under a canopy playing music on native instruments.

The boat captain, an overweight Hawaiian, guided the boat around the island, past a top-secret naval base on the island's northwest side, then toward the isolated Napoli cliffs. The volcanic formations rose from the sea nearly straight up. Wave erosion had created caves at the cliff bottoms; ancient Hawaiian kings were buried at the top of the cliffs. "In preparation for battle, Hawaiian warriors paddled war canoes into these caves. They raised their weapons to the ceiling and drank water as it trickled down from the graves of their dead kings," the Zodiac captain explained. Desmond drank the same water!

The trip's climax was the farewell party. Desmond had heard that on a previous Waterman trip to Greece, the CEO arrived at the event wearing a toga and riding upon a golden chariot driven by a team of four white horses. He knew this party would be fabulous. The event was staged at a sugar mill that had been abandoned for decades. The walls were painted over with graffiti. A storage tank was converted to a bar and dance area. Rusted trucks and equipment were lit with backlights and filled with smoke. Artificial flames made the top floors of the mill appear to be on fire; a few real fires were burning here and there for effect. At the front of the main stage was a cage where girls danced in leather skirts behind fence wire, highlighted by smoke and spotlights. A high-energy rock band was playing Springsteen hits.

WS hired the same advertising agency used successfully by Davidson Motorcycles, a company once near bankruptcy. The agency had produced a number of memorable Waterman ads featuring a bull in a china shop, and a bull walking down Wall Street. "We are bullish on capitalism," they proudly announced. They also planned the Kauai party. Party guests were given fake tattoos and American flag bandanas; women were urged to wear leather pants and tight tops.

Customized Davidson motorcycles, shipped from California, lined each side of the entrance. Bikers in leather jackets revved their motors as guests entered the party. To Desmond's ear the famous exhaust note sounded like "potato, potato, potato, potato." The ad agency figured they could promote Davidson motorcycles and Waterman Securities at the same event, most likely double billing both companies. "Wanna sit on my bike, honey? Want something big and powerful between your legs?" The agency hired real bikers. These guys were not party props or actors.

The smoke, motorcycle noise, fire, music, graffiti, and girls in cages created the atmosphere of a "B" movie set. It was like the aftermath of a nuclear holocaust, and the only people left alive were bikers, Waterman brokers, and wild chicks. The party continued, alcohol flowed, and the band played nonstop. After a dance, Karen and Desmond walked back to their table. "Karen, will you marry me?" Desmond surprised Karen while on one knee. He'd hidden the ring in the table centerpiece. "Yes, of course I will," she said without hesitation. A loud cheer went up as everyone stopped to watch the romantic proposal.

"Some of the guys rented a luxury limo bus and plan to tour the island to see the holiday decorations. In honor of our engagement, they invited us!" Desmond excitedly told Karen.

"If you enjoyed this party, just wait until the decorations tour. It's our greatest tradition. You will love it, great fun!" Desmond was told.

Desmond and Karen took their seats on the bus as others climbed aboard, bringing their own bottles of preferred beverage. It was a wild ride, with women flirtatiously straddling their dates' laps and giggling as the bus jerked and bumped over the back roads of Kauai. "Hit more bumps," a woman said to the driver, her dress pulled high and her legs spread apart, a bottle of tequila in her right hand. In the back of the bus, men were arguing over who had the biggest "cock." A woman decided to resolve the matter, pulling her black dress down, exposing her large breasts. "Can't accurately judge the biggest dick unless they're hard!" she said. The driver did not head in the direction of town. He was heading west, toward the island's poorest neighborhoods.

The fun and mayhem grew as the bus rolled along. "My god, look at that!" Everyone moved to that side of the bus to see a plastic Santa fastened to the roof of a small shack. "Over here, look at this! Homemade yard art!" It went on and on like this for hours. It was not a holiday tour of elaborate and expensive displays of lights. It was a heartbreaking display of human nature at its worst, intending to make fun of those less fortunate for the entertainment of a few privileged drunks. Desmond and Karen did not like this side of success; they felt ill. Desmond wondered what they would have said about his childhood home, decorated with tinfoil on the front door and an artificial drugstore Christmas tree in the window! They would have had a big laugh. Desmond did not want to "fit in" with these idiots.

The next morning, Karen and Desmond unsuccessfully nursed hangovers with coffee and cold showers. For souvenirs they collected a few of the seashell beads used as "do not disturb" signs on room doors. Another broker collected the free beads and used them as gifts for office employees. Karen and Desmond found a small Catholic chapel in Princeville on the east side of the island. The priest agreed to marry them that day. He loved "romantic stories," he said. It was a small ceremony with a few friends. The next day Karen returned to finish the remaining months of her navy enlistment in Chicago, and Desmond returned home to New Orleans. Almost nine months to the day, Isabella was born.

8

DESMOND UNDERSTOOD THE IMPACT OF politics and government regulations on financial markets. He knew government policies could determine the difference between an average job in the New Orleans Waterman office or a remarkable career as a financial rain maker. Desmond plotted to build political power. He researched Louisiana politics and explored the possibility of running for public office.

"Mr. Brandages, I would like to run for a seat in the Louisiana Senate," Desmond said.

Desmond discussed the reasons why he thought he could win. Mr. Brandages listened carefully and then explained that many brokers over the years had run for public office. "It is a great way to build a business quickly. You get name exposure, and the media promotes your business. It's a win-win situation. Why do you think so many lawyers run for office? It creates legitimacy and publicity. Politicians knock on every door, introduce themselves, and always leave a business card. Average people want to know celebrities; it makes them feel important. They would rather do business with a big shot rather than an unknown," he said.

Desmond completed the Outside Business Interest (OBI) forms required to obtain company permission for outside political activities. With the support of Mr. Brandages and the company's blessing,

Desmond qualified as a candidate for the Fourth Senate District seat from the New Orleans suburbs.

Desmond campaigned tirelessly and overcame many disadvantages to stage a remarkable come-from-behind election victory, beating a college president and a union boss as well. "Desmond Dupree, at twenty-four, is the youngest person ever elected to a major office in the state of Louisiana," announced a New Orleans newspaper.

"Desmond Dupree, please report to the manager's office."

Mr. Brandages was waiting for him at his office door. "Come in, Desmond." He related a conversation he had with the Waterman Legal and Compliance Division. "We have a problem. It appears the firm does substantial business in the Louisiana municipal bond market. Your Senate election creates a clear conflict of interest for Waterman," he said in a straightforward, no-nonsense way.

"Why was this not brought up before the election, for crying out loud?" Desmond asked.

"They approved the election campaign because no one expected you to win. They thought this was a publicity stunt," Mr. Brandages explained.

There were only two options: resign from the Senate or from WS. "I am sorry, Desmond, there is no other apparent solution. I need your decision by tomorrow."

Desmond would look foolish resigning from the elected position before even taking the oath of office, especially after receiving over one hundred thousand votes. The painful decision could go only one way. He loved working at Waterman Securities and knew he would regret the decision to resign.

Considering his financial experience, Desmond was appointed to the Banking and Lending Committee as a junior member. He helped oversee all Minimum Foundation Dollars, 8G, university funding, highway construction funding, and all general state operating expenses. However, as a junior member, he did not have control over banks, investment regulations, or mortgage regulations. Desmond positioned himself between two competing political factions. He became a decisive swing vote on many issues, including Senate leadership elections.

Desmond did not have the support to win higher leadership positions on his own. He could, however, help decide the winners. Dorothy, a candidate for Senate president, was blinded by political ambition and most likely to meet Desmond's needs. "I want the chairmanship of the Banking and Lending Committee and the chairmanship of the Subcommittee on Real Estate and Mortgages. I also want all legislation regarding mortgage issues, lending supervision, state bank charters, and bond funding directed to my Banking Committee," Desmond demanded without hesitation.

Dorothy said it was a ridiculous request. "This is impossible! No state gives that kind of financial political power to one individual chairmanship! It would be crazy to attempt! Are you fucking nuts?" she asked. "Do you want to run the world? What about the moon, or Jupiter? Anything else you want while we're at it?" she asked sarcastically.

"The question is how badly do you want to be the first female president of the Louisiana Senate?" Desmond asked.

Dorothy, a north Louisiana Baptist, would rather eat broken glass than give a New Orleans Catholic politician control over North Louisiana financial issues. He knew there was a chance he was overplaying his hand, but Desmond was not afraid.

Desmond had been an altar boy at Saint Dominic's Catholic Church for five years and attended Catholic schools from the third grade through high school. The first Latin phrase he memorized was *"Passio Christi, conforta me."* Desmond's faith would lead him through life's most difficult struggles. "Passion of Christ, comfort me," he repeated often during good and bad times. Dorothy underestimated Desmond's determination to push his agenda with fearless confidence.

Do I want people to fear me or love me? In politics fear was much more effective.

Dorothy's husband, "Beer Boy," was a Baton Rouge lobbyist representing the Beer Brewers and Distributor's Association. He was famous for throwing wild parties for state officials, usually at the Pentagon Apartments near the capitol building. Beer Boy had a large tattoo of the Liberty Bell on his upper right arm.

Desmond was late for a meeting when he ran up the seldom used back stairs of the capitol building. The steps connected the governor's fourth-floor office with the House chamber. He was only a few feet from where Huey Long was shot in the 1930s, and bullet holes were still evident in the marble walls and floor. Desmond opened the door to the second-floor landing and saw Beer Boy, who had someone pinned against the wall. Her skirt was pulled up around her waist, and her legs were wrapped around his hips. They were screwing in the darkness. The noise of someone hurrying up the stairs startled the lovers. "My god, someone's coming!" a female voice said. Desmond did not see her face, but he did recognize her well-known voice.

The governor had numerous health problems, including diabetes, and his inability to maintain an erection was well known. The governor had reassigned a state trooper to the Louisiana/Arkansas border for allegedly having sex with the First Lady in the governor's mansion. Desmond admired her fair complexion, red hair, and natural beauty. He wondered what she saw in the fat and arrogant beer salesman. If she needed companionship, Desmond wondered why he had not been chosen. He thought it would be really something to sleep with the governor's wife. How could anyone respect the governor when his wife was running around?

"Senator Dupree, wait, wait! This is not what you think!" shouted Beer Boy.

He rushed toward Desmond, pulling something from his pocket. "How much do you want? How about a beer distributor's fund-raiser at the Pentagon Apartments for your reelection campaign fund?" Beer Boy was peeling hundred-dollar bills from a thick roll. "You can keep a secret, right? You wouldn't tell anyone, right?"

The governor's wife walked past, adjusting her bra. Desmond caught a glimpse of her still-erect pink nipples, like the erasers on a fat elementary school pencil.

"Take care, Senator Desmond," she said with a wink, licking her upper lip. She ignored Beer Boy. Her hand brushed against Desmond's as she exited the room.

"The only person in Louisiana not screwing that crazy bitch is the governor!" The beer salesman wiped sweat from his forehead with a handkerchief. "If you are going to die from a heart attack anyway, it should be while fucking!" he said.

Desmond went to his meeting.

When Desmond arrived home, a call was waiting from the owner of the Baton Rouge Dive Shop. He had already called earlier in the day. "Would you like to have a certified diver's license?" he asked. Desmond had always been interested in scuba diving but thought it was a terribly dangerous hobby. The caller described his Baton Rouge location's success, the certifications of his instructors, and the thrill of scuba diving, especially in the coral formations common in the Caribbean. "We do our check-out dives at Harbor Island. Water is crystal clear for hundreds of feet!" he said. Desmond admired the caller's prospecting skills, but it had been a long day. He was not in the mood for phone solicitations.

"You don't understand!" the caller insisted. "You have been selected to receive our entire program, start to finish, all inclusive, including the equipment and travel, free of charge. This is a seventy-five-hundred-dollar value!"

Desmond was waiting for the hook. "I guess you want a credit card number, maybe my social security number, bank account, right?" he asked.

Since Desmond was an elected official, he was considered a "center of influence" and could help send more business to the Baton Rouge Dive Shop, according to the caller. "This is how we advertise," he said.

"Why was my name selected? Baton Rouge is full of elected officials," Desmond commented.

"Beer Boy suggested I call you."

Desmond was skilled at reading between political lines. The Dive Shop operated a dummy non-profit environmental organization supporting clean water. The organization was supported by the Beer Brewers and Distributor's Association. Beer Boy used the Dive Shop to reward friendly politicians with lavish "dive-trip" vacations. All very neat and tidy, no one paying bribes, no one accepting kickbacks, and credit was earned for supporting the environment.

Desmond made an appointment with Beer Boy. "I appreciate the dive school deal, but I have a better proposal for you." Although Desmond was nervous, he knew it usually did not show. *Passion of Christ, comfort me*, he said to himself. Avoiding small talk, Desmond went straight to the point. "I expect your help convincing Dorothy to support certain committee appointments."

Beer Boy's face turned red with anger. "Dorothy has nothing to do with this. Are you blackmailing me? Fuck you!" he said.

Desmond was offering an opportunity to solve everyone's problems. He stared directly into Beer Boy's eyes, hoping sweat was not soaking through his jacket. He repeated to himself, *Passio Christi, conforta me.*

"Your wife is the least of your problems. If the governor finds out the First Lady of Louisiana is screwing a beer salesman, you will be raising chickens in Bolivia for the rest of your life, that's if you're lucky," Desmond said.

Beer Boy dabbed his sweaty forehead with a handkerchief. "I guess you got me. What exactly do you need Dorothy to do?"

At the next Senate meeting, Dorothy had a surprising change of heart. "I do not know what is going on with my husband, but it better be worth it," she told Desmond.

Desmond became one of the most powerful members of the Louisiana Senate. He had nearly complete control over most state fiscal matters; most importantly, all issues involving real estate regulations.

Desmond developed a plan to create personal wealth. Exploiting real estate laws for personal gain seemed almost too easy, especially subprime and vacation condominium markets. "Bundling a variety of discounted, underperforming subprime loans together somehow allows them to be offered with an AAA credit rating. They move from a price discount to a price premium just like that. It's financial magic!" Desmond explained to Karen. "We are going to be rich!"

But Desmond's political career was to be short-lived, falling almost as quickly as his star rose. His greatest challenge was his own inability to wait patiently for the right opportunity. His youthful ambition and inexperience blinded him to the reality of his fragile political situation. Desmond foolishly trusted members of his own party. They viewed him as competition, especially older party members, who felt they had paid political dues for years. They resented Desmond's quick success; an "interloper," they called him. They would destroy Desmond's political career rather than risk upsetting their old boy's club and jeopardizing their own personal ambition.

Political loss was okay because Desmond believed he would capitalize on his unique experience handling large sums of public funds. He would reenter the investment banking world, a career he never actually left. His licenses were "parked" at a small municipal trading company to keep them active. During his time as an elected official, he managed public funds while avoiding legal troubles, a feat most unusual in Louisiana politics. He also learned to stand his ground. Desmond never backed down, even when pressured by determined and powerful opponents. He knew investment bankers had to be mean and nasty with a killer, "take no prisoner" attitude. Like lawyers, no company wants a nice investment banker. Desmond was now ready to make some real money.

9

DESMOND AND KAREN PURCHASED AN inexpensive weekend home in Pensacola, Florida. His family had vacationed there when he was young. Desmond's dad saved a few dollars each week until he had enough cash to take a Friday and Monday off and spend four summer days at the beach. The family's old Chevy station wagon did not have air-conditioning, but Desmond loved riding with the windows down, especially at night. He looked forward to these short beach vacations and loved the saltwater and white sand. Desmond also chose to buy a Florida panhandle home because he saw remarkable opportunities in the hot beachfront real estate markets there and wanted to be a part of it.

The quality of life in New Orleans spiraled downward for years. When the Dupree family was at the Pensacola weekend home, no one wanted to return to New Orleans. On a Sunday evening Desmond surprised Karen. "Why don't you and Isabella stay here? I'll commute back and forth on the weekends."

Desmond planned to land an investment banking position in Pensacola, sell the family property in New Orleans, and transfer to Pensacola within five years. The plan worked for only six months. One evening, Desmond reached Pensacola at about 8:00 Friday night. He opened the front door and stepped inside, especially eager to see Isabella. She toddled toward her mother, wrapped her little arms around her mother's leg, looked away from Desmond, and began to cry. Isabella was afraid of the father she did not recognize. Desmond's heart broke.

On Monday morning he called a New Orleans real estate broker. "I don't care what you get for the property. Sell it. Sell it all, sell it now! Sell everything!" Property values in New Orleans had been weak for years. Buyers were scarce. Desmond sold his New Orleans property at a significant loss. It would take years to dig out of this financial mudslide. Bankruptcy was out of the question since investment bankers are expected to know how to handle money. If you can't manage your own money, how can you manage your clients'? A blemish on Desmond's credit would ruin his career prospects.

Out of financial necessity Desmond accepted the first Pensacola job offer he received. The Dupree family's cash position was low, leaving no time to be selective. Steven Jones Investments was a quirky retail investment firm based in the Midwest that operated one-person branches in small towns throughout the country. They usually hired the local school principal or retired high school football coach to help them pass the Series 7 exam. Many Steven Jones brokers held only high school diplomas. Most had graduated from public schools; some had earned community college degrees. The company built a business opening ten-thousand-dollar IRAs and picking up small accounts overlooked by the major New York investment banks. Like vacuum cleaner salesmen, their brokers were trained to go door to door, soliciting the accounts of housewives.

Each individual Steven Jones branch required a branch office administrator (BOA) to run the office, computers, printers, communications equipment, property leases, and numerous other capital expenses. This wasteful cost structure, duplicated for each of the firm's nine thousand single-person branches, proved expensive. Desmond had previously balanced complicated budgets by consolidating entire state budgets and cutting overhead expenses. But this business plan did not add up. "How can Steven Jones possibly earn a profit?" Desmond asked a general partner during a visit to the St. Louis home office.

"Have you ever seen a bumblebee fly? Science says they should not be able to, but we know they do! Worry about the profitability of your branch. Don't worry about things above your pay grade," he told Desmond.

Steven Jones was a limited partnership and as such was not required to file financial reports like publicly traded investment banks. The financials remained a firm secret known only to the 288 general partners.

Desmond's small office consists of two rooms and a reception area. It was painted dark green and tan, with rugs and wall art he provided. He ditched the cheap company wall hangings, including a framed portrait of the managing partner and a complimentary print of the St. Louis skyline.

His BOA was a crazy old woman who had been employed with Steven Jones for thirty-five years, long past her prime. She had almost nothing to do until Desmond arrived. She resented his high expectations and increased workload requirements.

"Desmond Dupree is not what you think. He's having an affair," the BOA alleged in a handwritten letter she mailed to Karen. The Steven Jones Human Resources department refused to fire her, even though Desmond had the original signed letter as evidence. "It is not easy to terminate a loyal employee of thirty-five years," they said.

Each morning Desmond drove a different route or circled the block a few times before parking. He hated the dead-end nature of his current circumstances in this small office with a crazy assistant. It took all his strength just to start each day.

After a period of time Desmond's office was profitable and climbing the roster of the firm's most successful branches. He built the business without calling upon any of his Louisiana Senate connections. "This is Desmond Dupree with Steven Jones. I'm new to the area and working to build my business. Do you currently have anyone handling your investments?" He made two hundred of these calls each day. He joined the Rotary, Jaycees, Chamber of

Commerce, and Business Round Tables. Desmond wanted to prove he could go to a new city and earn a living.

He wrote a weekly article for the local newspaper, discussing various financial and economic issues. The articles, well received, created a sense of legitimacy and expert knowledge as Desmond worked to open accounts. He also announced the morning market update at 8:00 on a local FM radio station. This made Desmond a local radio celebrity.

Desmond followed careful scripts and guidelines with clear compliance rules limiting on-air discussions to financial subjects. But the crazy BOA called the St. Louis compliance department. "Desmond is discussing politics on the market update broadcast." It was his word against hers because the radio station did not maintain broadcast recordings. Desmond spent hours answering questions from a suspicious company attorney. "I consider my political views to be a private, personal matter," Desmond said. Nevertheless, he paid a fine and was required to keep and maintain recordings for every daily broadcast. He sent these tapes to St. Louis lawyers each month, an expensive and arduous task.

Desmond did not take his punishment personally, but the incident did demonstrate how difficult it was to fairly enforce compliance rules from a distance. Steven Jones used BOAs as a type of company police force reporting on the activity of brokers. Receiving no specific compliance training or education, they created a Gestapo-like atmosphere, accumulating their own career accolades at the broker's expense.

10

ACCORDING TO PREHIRE FORMULAS, DESMOND
expected a large bonus, part of a profit-sharing plan for successful branches. He calculated the amount to be 56,000 dollars. The check was mailed to his home. It amounted to only 1,850 dollars. Desmond's profit before tax was redistributed, covering expenses of less profitable branches. His hard work was supporting lazy brokers in poorly performing branches. He now understood how this bumble-bee flew!

A "Good Knight" letter arrived along with the bonus check. Desmond learned he would be required to divide his hard-won accounts fifty-fifty with a new broker who was moving to the area and opening a new Steven Jones office nearby, competing directly with Desmond. In Steven Jones language, a "Good Knight" was an experienced broker riding to the rescue of a new hire for the overall benefit of the general partners. In return Desmond received eligibility for a company-sponsored trip. A five-day vacation to Disney World would cost Desmond nearly a million dollars in lost business over time. Desmond tried not to get upset. Anger was too exhausting. He needed to stay focused.

Desmond's résumé of unique experiences was eventually noticed by a premier Wall Street investment bank with a strong presence in Florida's real estate securities market. His prayers were answered in remarkable ways. *"Passio Christi, conforta me."* Timing was perfect.

Desmond would ride the oceanfront property craze to unbelievable prosperity and become a superstar in the securitized mortgages and collateralized mortgage obligations markets.

Desmond's Louisiana political experience provided ideal training for working effectively with government-sponsored enterprises (GSEs) Freddie Mac and Fannie Mae. The GSEs' responsibilities included securitizing the country's mortgages. He resigned from Steven Jones Investments by sending an email to his district leader in Andalusia, Alabama: "Please accept this notice as my resignation from Steven Jones, effective immediately. I appreciate your time and attention to this important notification."

The new recruit employment package was worthwhile, with an initial upfront bonus worth 120 percent of Desmond's trailing twelve-month production earnings. It was nearly half a million dollars. Additional backend bonuses were based on Desmond's success moving his clients to the new firm, coupled with expected revenue production for the next five years. This could add another one hundred percent, providing a comprehensive package worth nearly one million dollars.

The recruit deal structure appeared to be tax-free. The mechanism called a forgivable loan required equal repayments due once a year on Desmond's hire date. His contract called for a seven-year "repayment" schedule. On March eighth each year Desmond wrote a check for 71,500 dollars payable to his new firm. But approximately one week later, he received a check from the firm for 88,500 dollars as an additional bonus. The firm and Desmond swapped checks. Desmond paid taxes on the difference between 88,500 and the 71,500 dollars, a clever wash. His tax rate on one million dollars was less than five percent per year. The forgivable loan structure, the same for all backend bonuses, concluded all taxable obligations in seven years.

Steven Jones offered weak defense against departing brokers. Single-person branches were left vacant without licensed personnel available to assist clients or to retain business. They eventually sent a new broker, fresh from St. Louis training and eager to walk into a successful branch. But having no concept of how to build a business, rookie brokers would be no match for experienced professionals. Desmond's former district manager expected him to take twenty-five percent of client assets to his new firm. "Clients love Steven Jones. Who would move to a major wire house? I'm not worried," he said.

Like a schoolgirl with a crush, the district manager was blind to obvious weaknesses. Desmond aggressively pursued every client. He kept a list of other Steven Jones clients he had met. He called them as well. When asked why he was changing firms, he was always truthful. "My departure is no reflection upon Steven Jones, but this is a lucrative career offer I can't pass up!" Desmond also explained the key differences between a small regional retail organization and an international Wall Street investment bank. Successful people understood this logic and forthright honesty. He transferred a total of 115 percent of the firm's client assets to his new firm.

"This is not fair, all the assets are leaving. We need to do something!" the young broker assigned to Desmond's old Steven Jones office complained. He faced stacks of transfer documents each day. Desmond was a fierce competitor and wanted the new broker's testicles hanging above his living room mantel. Within a few months the Steven Jones office closed. Four months after that Desmond hit the first year bonus requirements, earning another 100,000-dollar forgivable loan.

Desmond began studying for the Series 9 and Series 10 financial management exams. These qualified him for financial sales supervision and as a registered options principal (ROP). He was told that there was only a remote chance a management opening would come along in the near future. Nevertheless, he would be prepared if the opportunity arose. It was difficult to work all day and study each evening. Sometimes with best intentions, he fell asleep after one paragraph or just a single sentence. Studying trading strategy books, puts, calls, covered and uncovered, spreads and straddles would be important risk management tools. Desmond read them over and over and learned as much as he could.

Karen did not understand Desmond's behavior. He was never around, and he seemed "detached and distant," she said. She did not understand the pressure and stress he was under since their financial future depended on his success in passing these two incredibly difficult exams. Desmond began to resent Karen's inability to understand how he made a living for them. The fact that she added more aggravation to his mounting stress was lost on her.

One Sunday afternoon, he asked Karen to take a ride with him. They drove around the expensive bay front area. "Do you want to live here?" Desmond asked. "I need to pass these exams. Give me some time. I only need a few more weeks, and then things will settle down, I promise." Desmond realized Karen had different motivations than he did. He believed she needed love and affection more than wealth. "I don't care where we live. I just need to know that I am the most important thing in your life," she said. Karen wanted love. Desmond wanted it all.

The weeklong study course in Atlanta summarized the information Desmond studied. Ralph, an operations manager for an independent Atlanta investment firm, needed the licenses for an important promotion. His firm offered a million-dollar bonus upon the successful completion of the Series 9 and Series 10 exams. Ralph left class early every day. He did not bother to sit in for the final review day. *I guess a million dollars is not as significant as it once was,* Desmond thought.

On the first attempt to pass the sales supervision exam, Desmond scored a sixty-nine, one point shy of passing. He scheduled a retake within thirty days and passed. The ROP exam, only offered in New Orleans, required leaving Pensacola at 4:00 a.m. Desmond drove through the night, making numerous coffee stops and using the large thirty-two-ounce cups intended for soft drinks. He was wide awake and ready to go when he reached the testing center in Metairie. Relaxed, confident, and ready, he walked up to the front desk. "I'm Desmond Dupree, here to take the Series 10 ROP exam."

The test administrator could not find Desmond's registration. She made phone calls. "I'm sorry, it seems you are scheduled at the other New Orleans testing center," she said with a concerned look. "No one can be admitted once the exam starts," she added, reminding Desmond to hurry. He ran to his car, sped to the other location on the south side of Metairie, and arrived with only moments to spare. Now stressed and aggravated, heart racing, he needed fifteen minutes to calm down.

He took a deep breath. "I got this!" he said over and over to himself. Desmond scored an eighty-six, an outstanding score on such a difficult test. He called Karen with the good news.

"Hurry home! I've never slept with an ROP before!" she said.

11

PUBLISHING A MONTHLY NEWSLETTER TO
attract prospective new clients made economic sense. This would help
promote Desmond's name, build his business, and enhance his repu-
tation as an investment banking professional. The firm's compliance
department would review and approve articles before printing, but
they did not bother to maintain a copy of the mailing lists. Desmond
wanted a new angle, something profitable but radically different from
"run of the mill" investment letters currently available. His market
letter would be the world's most accurate. Desmond's scheme was a
remarkably unique plan, beautiful in its simplicity.

In five weeks, Desmond believed he could generate nearly five
thousand potential subscribers. If each likely subscriber paid the five-
thousand-dollar annual subscription rate, then the newsletter would
generate twenty-five million dollars in fees. "Let's go see the new
BMWs!" Desmond called home to Karen. "Our financial troubles are
behind us!" he said. Karen was learning to appreciate Desmond's
financial magic. But was she loyal because she loved him or because
she was learning to love money? Desmond wondered. He knew
money was a powerful force but hoped Karen's devotion was still
rooted in loyalty.

In Dante's Inferno, hell is made up of various rings. Each populated by condemned souls. The center of hell is bitter cold since it is
far removed from God's warmth and affection. The innermost ring is

reserved for the worst of humanity. Not rapists, molesters, or murderers, as would be expected. Dante's inner ring is populated by the disloyal, like Brutus and Judas, condemned to spend all eternity gnawed upon by three-headed serpents, punishment for their disloyalty. Disloyalty was unforgivable in Desmond's view as well, the worst betrayal.

Articles in "Prosperity" covered everything from real estate investing to straddles on options, commodity plays, and exchange-traded funds. In the "Market Outlook" column, Desmond offered his predictions on the most significant market indexes.

He developed a 150,000-name list comprised of sophisticated investors. Each individual had a high net worth and aggressive trading record. These investors were called "whales." Desmond offered the first five-week trial subscription free. A five-thousand-dollar subscription fee was required to continue receiving the letter after that. Investment banking is a profession where greed is rewarded and encouraged. Markets convert the drive for individual wealth into the world's most successful economy, and everyone benefits. Each week, Desmond prepared two different versions of "Prosperity." Half his subscriber list received bullish views. The other half received a bearish outlook. Some articles were the same in both versions. The "Market Outlook" section was always different.

In the first mailing, Desmond sent seventy-five thousand letters predicting markets would go up. The other seventy-five thousand predicted markets would go down. "Action this week, by the Federal Reserve Bank, will cause the Dow to break out of its resistance level and move higher from here." The other subscribers received letters with the exact opposite prediction. "Action this week, by the Federal Reserve Bank, will cause the Dow to crash through support levels moving lower from here!" Desmond always provided detailed explanations supporting his predictions. Each week he removed the fifty percent of the mailing list who received letters with incorrect predictions. Desmond repeated this process for five weeks.

After the initial five-week period, Desmond's list was narrowed down to about five thousand likely "Prosperity" subscribers who believed he could accurately predict markets. "For the past five weeks, you received complimentary copies of 'Prosperity,' the world's most accurate investor newsletter! Each week 'Prosperity' correctly called market direction! How can anyone place a dollar value on information this accurate?" Desmond wrote. "For a limited time we are offering a subscription opportunity to a select group of high net worth, sophisticated investors like you!" More than three thousand investors sent checks. "Please find enclosed the five-thousand-dollar subscription fee. I have also enclosed a one-thousand-dollar check as an incentive to insure inclusion in your limited offer," wrote a hopeful subscriber fighting for a valuable spot on Desmond's mailing list.

"Prosperity" earned over fifteen million dollars. Not a bad payday for five weeks of work. Desmond planned to invest in Florida real estate. He was concerned with keeping and growing wealth, not spending it on frivolous things.

The Pensacola real estate market seemed ready for growth. The first wave of baby boomers were reaching retirement with fat 401(k)s, second homes, and investment accounts. Investment banks devised entire investment programs targeted specifically at this group. Hiring goals for investment firms changed as well; it was unlikely for anyone to land a Wall Street job upon college graduation. Retiring boomers wanted to sit across the table from someone who remembered moon shots, Watergate, Nixon, and the Cold War. They were unlikely to do business with a twenty-something. National ad campaigns played the music of Woodstock with Boomers driving restored VW vans with surfboards on top. "This generation won't go out in a rocking chair. They have a plan!" the commercials claimed. The children of the greatest generation, the most prosperous generation, had a plan as well. They wanted to own Florida real estate.

Investment fortunes are made following society's major trends. In the 1950s, fortunes were made investing in baby food and baby products as the population exploded. Next, hotel chains sprang up along the new interstate highway system as Americans spent their leisure time traveling. In the late 1960s and into the '70s, Boomers' children began careers, also making and spending money as consumers. By the early 1980s they were having their own families, and the cycle was starting again. Empty-nesters buying vacation investment real estate and second homes in Florida were the next major trend.

12

PLANNING TO INVEST TEN MILLION dollars in beachfront condominium projects from Pensacola to Gulf Shores, Desmond began by buying up old single-story, "mom and pop" quaint motels. Once popular, they were now an inefficient use of valuable beachfront real estate. The old hotels were demolished, clearing the way for modern luxury condo high-rise towers.

Desmond wanted a team of loyal associates. If he trusted someone, he would stay with them, even if they made mistakes. "Dance with the one who brung you!" he believed. Desmond knew stories of wealthy individuals who wanted everyone around them to be successful as well. He was never jealous of another's success if they were on his team, following his lead. If not on his team, he tried to find out what they were doing. Beating them at their own game was his goal.

On the other hand, one of Desmond's former investment clients owned an automobile dealership with salesmen working on straight commission. Desmond had always baked his own financial bread, respecting salesmen's willingness to take risks associated with variable-income jobs. The owner hated to write monthly commission checks. "These bastards make more money than me. I should fire these pricks and sell the cars myself!" he complained.

"That is all wrong! You should love to write those checks. The more your salesmen make, the more you do," Desmond tried to explain. He was unable to teach the owner to control his ego. Soon thereafter the dealership was liquidated.

Dr. Saul "Sonny" Goldstein owned a Pensacola mortgage broker-age business, a title company, a finance company, and an insurance agency, together called the Goldstein Group. The Group was such a powerful force that a number of major lenders allowed Sonny to do his own underwriting. The mortgage business sent clients to the title and insurance companies. The title company and the insurance agency sent clients to the mortgage company. They all sent business to the finance company, creating a web of conflicting interest. Sonny operated mortgage offices in the lobbies of prominent real estate firms. Giving cash bird-dog fees to agents enabled Sonny to expand his business quickly. Nothing happened in local real estate without his knowledge.

Dr. Sonny earned a PhD in Economics from Columbia College and was chairman of the University of Northwest Michigan, Department of Economics, where he remained a Professor Emeritus. His hair was now long, his face unshaven, and he listened to Jamaican beach music too much. "I want to meet the big man spending ten million dollars on Pensacola property. I have a proposal which should be of interest. How about tomorrow morning," Dr. Sonny asked Desmond. "See you tomorrow," Desmond replied. The line went dead as Sonny turned his Mercedes convertible into the Sunset Bay Marina parking lot.

Desmond's timing in the Pensacola real estate market was almost perfect. He bought the best properties just as prices began to spiral upward. Dr. Sonny proposed using the Goldstein Group to finance and market Desmond's real estate deals. "We pre-sell condo units and bundle the entire package as real-estate-backed bonds. The bonds receive the highest AAA ratings because we combine parts of many different condo developments, pooling them together in one invest-ment. Any single default or foreclosure cannot hurt the overall bond values," Dr. Sonny explained. "There is little financial danger. The possibility of each development failing at the same time is extremely unlikely. You have a greater chance of being struck by lightning twice in a single day. Also, risk is spread between numerous individuals and various condo developments," he continued. "The financing structure allows us to diversify risk even further as the bonds can be marketed internationally. This creates an ever-expanding pool of funds to invest in additional property, igniting more demand."

Sonny was convincing, like a college professor. "Remember the simple rules of supply and demand and equilibrium price. Beachfront property is limited and highly desirable. It is the supermodel pussy of real estate. High demand will certainly cause prices to explode upwards. We, my friend, will hire people just to count our cash! Years from now, your grandchildren will raise a toast to you while sailing to Nantucket."

Dr. Sonny was persuasive, but he was unaware of Desmond's political and financial experience. Desmond quietly listened. Sonny could be useful.

A condominium offering statement and sales material was developed for each of Desmond's proposed properties. Architectural drawings showed floor plans, elevations, and amenities. Each page was clearly marked "NEED NOT BE BUILT." This disclosure provided Desmond and Dr. Sonny the right to return escrow deposits and scrap the project if necessary. "The disclosure is there as a routine matter, like an airbag in your car. You may never need it, but it is there," Dr. Sonny said. He went through the offering documents page by page, pointing out legal language protecting Desmond from loss. "It is impossible to lose money," Dr. Sonny promised.

"Why would any investor accept these terms?" Desmond asked, although he already knew the answer.

"They are greedy!" was Sonny's response. Potential investors could purchase condominium units preconstruction, with ten percent down or a letter of credit guaranteeing the unpaid balance. Actual closings took place when the buildings were completed. Conveniently, letters of credit could be obtained from Sonny's finance company.

Prices increased as soon as construction began, creating a preconstruction goldmine for early investors. Most units were "flipped" seven or eight times before the ultimate buyer closed on the deal. Each successive investor bid prices higher and higher. Sonny and Desmond always held ten to fifteen percent of the units for themselves at preconstruction prices.

Most developments sold out within a day or two of the initial announcement. The "flipping" began as soon as all available preconstruction units were sold. A single three-bedroom condo selling for five hundred thousand dollars preconstruction could easily double in price when completed. Desmond watched the value of his assets increase at a remarkable pace. He was becoming a very wealthy person, on paper.

Real-estate-backed bonds were easy to package and sell to Wall Street. The condominium developments increased in value quickly, enhancing the collateral backing the bonds. With escalating prices, the AAA ratings were assured. These high ratings allowed the condominiums to be funded at the lowest possible interest rates, further increasing demand.

Investors wanted in because credit ratings were high. The ratings were high because more and more investors wanted in the game. Desmond's developments carried the same rating as government-sponsored enterprises like Freddie Mac and Fannie Mae. They, too, offered pooled mortgage bonds. Desmond's firm and other major Wall Street investment banks were eager to provide additional AAA real estate opportunities for their clients, driving demand even stronger.

13

DESMOND'S MAILBOX, LOCATED AT THE street, was a pleasant stroll from his front door. Under shady oaks he sorted the mail, discarding the unwanted solicitations while retaining the envelopes worth another look. A colorful piece of junk mail caught his eye. "What is this?" A real estate seminar invitation guaranteeing a three hundred percent annual return was hand-addressed to Desmond. The organization sponsoring the seminar called itself "Flipper." Only an idiot would put such a ridiculous guarantee in writing. Sending it out in a mass market mailing was incredibly foolish. Desmond was impressed by the handwritten address, but its effectiveness was diminished by the bulk-rate stamp. Amateurs, no doubt!

There were certain words Desmond would never use, and "guarantee" was at the top of the list. Although compliance officers allowed "guaranteed" to be used in relation to direct obligations of the US Treasury, Desmond believed the word always led to litigation. "Words like that are the reason lawyers can send their kids to private schools," he said.

With every seat taken, late arrivals were standing against the walls, some still waiting outside to sign up. Desmond stood near the door with his arms folded, planning a quick exit and dinner with Karen. Attractive girls at the registration table, the professional nature of the handout materials, and condominium drawings on easels designed to illustrate the good life convinced him to hang around.

It is true one will never see unattractive people in boat, car, or beachfront property ads. Buy this or that and you can live an exciting life, is the unspoken message. In a certain sense that is exactly what Flipper was selling—dreams. Looking around the room, Desmond could see that some attendees were obviously experienced "whales." Others were dreamers about to risk their life savings on a hopeless attempt to escape desperate lives.

Desmond could easily pick out the "marks" by their eager looks, costume jewelry, drugstore cologne, and cheap suits. "Marks" asked questions like, "What is the minimal investment allowed, and do we have to pay association fees?" This was a target-rich environment, mosquitoes at a nudist colony. In this situation, if you didn't know who the "marks" were, you probably were one. Like a freshman coed dating the varsity quarterback, someone was going to get screwed. The outcome was never in doubt. In financial pornography, someone always got screwed.

The lights dimmed. The song "Easy Living" by Uriah Heep played on the overhead speakers. Desmond loved the song's lyrics: "Ready for my happy day and some easy living. I've been forgiven." Uriah Heep's other great hit from the '70s was "Stealin' When I Should Have Been Buyin'." Desmond enjoyed the irony. Two attractive young female lawyers in tight skirts and a middle-aged finance man walked onto the stage. "This is a unique and exclusive opportunity. Having been carefully selected from a list of potential investors, you will learn proprietary information which should not be shared with others." Many in the audience bobbed their heads in agreement. They looked at their spouses with eager anticipation, believing that their ships were finally coming in.

The lawyers reviewed the planned condominium developments from Panama City, Florida, to Orange Beach, Alabama, and pointed to the computer-generated photos lining the walls. On the front row, one individual already had his checkbook out, although Desmond suspected he must be a Flipper operative. "This is different from any other opportunity available. We can offer a guaranteed return because we have a significant relationship with the most successful developer in the state," the presenters claimed.

Photos of the Flipper representatives in hard hats surveying construction sites with a representative of Batts Construction evidenced the unique relationship. In each photo was Robert Batts, son of the firm's founder. Desmond figured the son allowed the use of his name so he could play around with the eager Flipper female lawyers. They probably had hot threesomes in top-floor penthouses of the condos Batts Construction built. Ah, the good life! Easy living! Who could blame them?

"The demand for new construction is outrageous. Most individual investors will never have the opportunity to get in on the ground floor, unless they know someone." The unpleasant truth was explained. "Small investors are buying properties today which have already been flipped three or four times. Paying thousands more than the initial offering price, they are making other people rich. We have the solution!" They set the hook. "We have connections with Batts Construction. This guarantees our investors the best deals first on the best properties anywhere on the beach," the finance man stated.

"The minimal initial investment required is one hundred thousand dollars, which can be secured with cash or a second lien against homes and property." The lawyers assured everyone the units would resell at a profit. Asked to invest based on sketches and promises, in return investors actually owned nothing, only shares of Flipper Inc. The company legally owned the individual condo units. It was unclear to Desmond if investors actually owned anything tangible at all.

Desmond read the small print carefully. Flipper took a thirty percent upfront fee for administration charges and as compensation for their connection with a successful property developer. The remaining seventy percent would be used to purchase the investments as promised. But all property was titled in the name of Flipper Inc., and all shares of the company were owned by a small group of principals.

Actual investor capital depreciated faster than if they had bought a new Lincoln Town Car.

Fifteen individuals wrote hundred-thousand-dollar checks. Shoving and pushing, each wanting to be the first to hand over their money. The scene reminded Desmond of small-town high school graduations. The new grads immediately rush to the town mill employment office to be first on the list for new hires, trying to secure lifetime employment. Flipper earned one and a half million dollars for a ninety-minute presentation. Many attendees left disappointed because they could not come up with the minimal amount. They promised to call friends and relatives, trying to retain participation commitments until they could raise money. "No pay, no play!" the finance man said.

Desmond saw other signs the real estate market was becoming dangerously inflated, a classic asset bubble, a modern "tulip mania." In the 1630s, enthusiasm for the Dutch flowers triggered a speculative frenzy. Some single bulbs sold for more than gold and diamonds.

Wayne was the local barber who cut Desmond's hair. Every two-dollar bill he had ever received was tacked to the walls of his shop. The barbershop, populated with a unique cast of local characters and self-proclaimed experts in various fields, including international relations and economics, was a cultural treasure. The local newspaper ran a series of articles about "Wayne's World."

"I figure I'm worth about three million dollars," Wayne said to Desmond. He owned a few acres outside of town that had recently been used as a pig farm. "A big developer from Atlanta has been sniffing around. Yes sir, three million," Wayne exclaimed.

An old man reading a *Playboy* magazine explained why Wayne would be a fool to accept such a "lowball offer." He put the magazine down. "The Chinese haven't started buying yet. The Atlanta developer is only going to resell to the Chinks. Don't be a fool, Wayne! You should sell to the Chinks yourself, cut out the middleman!" he explained with complete confidence. Desmond did not say much because when Wayne got excited, he gave bad haircuts. He did wonder why someone worth three million dollars still cut hair every day.

According to the local real estate board, Pensacola to Gulf Shores had more than four thousand registered full-time agents and at least that many working part time. Orange Beach had more than two agents for each listed property. Real estate "schools" operated by real estate brokers offered night classes to working folks eager to change careers. They charged ridiculous tuition rates preparing people to earn a license by passing a simple test. The parking lots were always full.

These brokers made more money teaching real estate than selling it. During the California gold rush, merchants selling blue jeans and equipment made more than the prospectors. Nurses, electricians, mechanics were all ready to give up good jobs to chase easy money, pie-in-the-sky dreams. Everything was getting dangerously out of hand. Desmond began considering plans to cash out. He could already be too late.

14

DR. SONNY EXPLAINED, "THE COMMUNITY
Reinvestment Act intended to make home ownership easily available.
Legislation, a powerful tool, forced banks to make mortgage loans in
neighborhoods with declining home values. These mortgages had
lower standards, down payments, and underwriting guidelines. Still,
the Community Reinvestment goals were worthwhile. Neighborhoods with high levels of home ownership usually offer a better quality of life, stronger communities, and higher property values.

"The law did more than push banks into fair lending agreements.
Ultimately it created situations which eliminated lending standards
across the board. Once standards were lowered for subprime borrowers, banks extended the low underwriting guidelines to all borrowers."
He took another sip of his drink. "The well-intentioned law gave
banks regulatory cover, creating the subprime mortgage market. Freddie Mac and Fannie Mac, under increasing political pressure, packaged more and more high-risk mortgages. Millions of individual
high-risk mortgages, rated as AAA government bonds, were processed
and sold each year. We have simply taken advantage of the situation.
Nothing wrong with that!"

Desmond's parents paid fourteen thousand dollars for the family
home back in 1963. The mortgage was held by the Guarantee Homestead and Loan Bank (GHLB) on Canal Street in New Orleans. Each
month, for thirty years, Desmond's dad drove the family station

wagon down to the Guarantee Homestead office to make the monthly payments. The mortgage was the first bill paid each month. Thirty years was a very long time, with many economic ups and downs. Desmond's dad made every payment in full and on time. He kept a small booklet showing a credit for each payment in one column, the declining principal balance in another. The teller's initials who processed each payment were on the right. He kept the booklet in a fireproof box hidden under the bed. The neighborhood banker is gone now, relegated to dusty memories of a simpler time.

By 1994, the Dupree family home was finally owned free and clear. In that year five percent of all mortgages were subprime, and thirty percent of those subprime loans were securitized. By 2006, nearly one quarter of all mortgages were subprime, and nearly ninety percent of them were securitized.

A recent immigrant in Florida, working as a fast-food restaurant manager, qualified to purchase a million-dollar condo. For two years he paid only interest. Then the rate adjusted higher with a one-million-dollar balloon payment due on month twenty-four. The fifty-thousand-dollar down payment he borrowed from friends and family went to cover fees and expenses. The real estate salesman, closing the deal in Spanish, printed all documents in English. This mortgage and many others like it were packaged into AAA-rated investments and sold to investors worldwide. They were injected into the arteries of the world financial system like cancer cells.

The Asian currency crises of the 1990s started in Thailand and quickly spread throughout Asia, Argentina, and Russia. Argentina devalued its currency, Russia defaulted on its national debt, and the once dynamic economies of many emerging markets faced financial disaster. The solution to stop the downward-spiraling currency devaluations was to peg foreign currency exchange rates to the US dollar. If the dollar remained strong, then the pegs were strong as well. These countries began accumulating dollar reserves to protect their currency. Dollars were held in the form of T-bills earning modest interest but guaranteeing the principal by the full faith and credit of the US government.

As the currency crises faded into history, central banks around the world began seeking higher returns for their massive US dollar holdings. Government-backed real estate bonds provided the sought-after returns. Emerging market economies began to grow with high interest payments earned from American real estate bonds rather than from domestic GDP growth. They used this easy money to fund consumption binges. It was not used to modernize their economies or become more competitive. Real estate bonds were bundled together, stamped with the US government's seal of approval, and then sold worldwide. Some of these bonds, sold in faraway places like Singapore, funded Desmond's beach developments in Gulf Shores, Alabama.

Credit agencies assigned AAA ratings to everything. The flood of money and growing demand seemed to be unending. A New York investment bank became the largest property owner in the world, surpassing the Catholic Church. The demand for real estate bonds continued growing, driving property values up like rocket fuel. Funding was available for nearly any project. Prudent due diligence took a backseat to the flood of speculative cash and greed washing over the country. It was like the whole country was taking a financial doughnut break from common sense.

Desmond knew any abrupt change of direction on Federal Reserve interest rate policy would be disastrous for the overheated real estate market. Bond prices have an inverse relationship to interest rates. If interest rates are going up, bond prices move down. When interest rates move down, bond prices move up.

After the September 11th attacks on the World Trade Center, the US economy slowed dramatically. In efforts to restart consumer spending, the Federal Reserve began aggressively lowering interest rates. Rates eventually fell to one percent. No new terrorist attacks followed, and eventually the economy began to stabilize. Lower interest rates meant buyers could afford more expensive homes. Foreclosures were less likely because payments were low. The increased demand drove prices up as home builders geared up to satisfy the demands of eager buyers with cheap money.

But the Federal Reserve Board has a duel mandate, fighting inflation and growing the economy. Concerned about low rates fueling
runaway inflation, the Federal Reserve chairman issued a surprise
warning. He said easy money was creating a climate of "irrational exuberance." Then he began raising rates at a blazingly fast pace, driving
them over five percent. Unexpected, the change of direction caught
real estate markets by surprise. Adjustable rate and nonstandard mortgages began defaulting first. When asked about the rising default
rates, the Federal Reserve chairman, trying to reassure nervous markets, said, "All we have here is a thirty-billion-dollar subprime problem. Not to worry!"

Desmond knew better. There was plenty to worry about. He quietly listed some of his properties. Poorly planned sales would drive
prices down further, so he could list only two or three properties in
each beachfront market at a time. Desmond was reluctant to set lower
prices because that could damage the comparables for his remaining
properties. He was already too late. Although the market still
appeared healthy on the surface, the reality was quite different. Massive revaluation and retraction of real estate assets worldwide were
already under way.

15

DESMOND HIRED SANDCASTLE REAL ESTATE
to handle his sales. The listed properties were placed on lockbox.
Agents could show the condos easily since the keys were available with
the lockbox code. Knowing that a number of showings were scheduled, and not wanting to interfere, Desmond planned his activities
around the sales calendar.

On a Tuesday afternoon he dropped by his favorite Orange Beach
property unannounced. He was in the area for a late lunch appointment. The condo was Isabella's favorite. It was used often for family
beach weekends. It was never placed on a rental program and was decorated as a personal residence. Desmond was surprised to find an
empty champagne bottle and two empty glasses on the table. *Perhaps
the condo was staged,* he thought. Agents sometimes do this so
prospective buyers can envision a certain lifestyle. Then he looked in
the bedroom.

"No one screws in my bed except me!" Desmond was outraged. A
middle-aged married agent and an out-of-town "investor" were using
his condo as a secret love nest. "Get the fuck out!" he demanded. The
startled lovers dressed quickly. "Take it easy, fella," the man said. As
an experienced businessman and politician, Desmond prided himself
on self-control. He never made emotional decisions. This was the one
exception to that rule. "I am pulling all my listings. I want every

damn sign you people have on my properties removed, today!"
Desmond screamed into his phone.

The managing partner of Sandcastle Real Estate pleaded with
Desmond to change his mind. "Mr. Dupree, we have pending ads
and MLS listings, very expensive," he said.

"Don't tell me about your problems. You should have thought
about that before your agents used my home as a brothel!" Desmond
said. This was not the time to pull listings; the market was losing
momentum quickly, and any sales delay could spell trouble.
Desmond was angry.

Real estate prices were in a free fall even before the "love nest" incident. Desmond was unable to sell fast enough. He found himself
holding property worth much less than he owed. Unable to pay delin-
quent construction bills, contractors placed liens on Desmond's
remaining properties. The liens made it even harder to sell properties
that were now encumbered. Bankruptcy was becoming an attractive
alternative as Desmond considered his options. Bankruptcy would
also mean the end of his career in the financial industry. Any filing
would violate terms of his management supervisory licenses.

How could things reverse so quickly? he wondered while driving his
Aston Martin convertible along the beach road. Foreclosure signs
were popping up everywhere. As bad as things seemed, these signs
were inaccurate indicators of the true severity of the market situation.
Most banks maintained a policy against placing foreclosure signs on
individual properties. They believed the signs invited vandalism and
encouraged further price devaluations.

Desmond's difficult predicament was a forward indicator of
unprecedented financial deterioration taking place on a worldwide
scale. America was a consumer-driven economy. After the real estate
crash, people stopped consuming. Manufacturing was the next economic domino to fall. Banks were losing trillions of dollars on
defaulted consumer loans and mortgages. They were unable to dis-
tribute these loans into the global economy quickly enough. A large
share of these losses fell upon Wall Street. Three of the five largest

firms were collapsing in scandal, disgrace, and confusion. Trust in America's financial institutions sank, encouraging a move away from any market risk.

Worldwide, the value of financial assets dropped by forty trillion dollars. Many financial institutions were rendered insolvent when their assets were marked to the deprecated market value. Businesses could not obtain financing, and employment collapsed. The hangover from America's free-spending financial orgy was felt from Europe to Asia and South America, redefining world order in devastating and unanticipated ways. The integrated web of global financial interdependency unraveled faster than the French army during World War II. This time there would be no Dunkirk flotilla to save us.

The real estate market was first to collapse, followed by sovereign debt issues of multiple countries. Then the US Treasury missed interest payments associated with a certain T-Bill series, triggering a technical default and credit downgrades. Smaller sovereign central banks around the globe were pushed into insolvency as they supported domestic banks harboring mountains of depreciating US bonds. The wealth of an entire generation disappeared overnight, including Desmond's.

16

AMERICA'S FINANCIAL DOWNFALL CAME QUICKLY.
Empires are not eternal. Signs of decline go unnoticed until the weight of accumulated obligations become unbearable. During desperate times citizens gladly exchange liberty for empty promises, eager to follow any charismatic charlatan. When cities are filthy, crime is rampant, and people are hungry, they don't worry about protecting constitutional rights. Thus the powerless are kept hungry, poor, and afraid, exploited by corrupt and cunning government interested only in satisfying its own greed, like a parasite within. Then scavengers appear. Buzzards feed upon the rotting carcass of the decaying empire. The scenario is always the same, with a final violent implosion as the dying empire takes its final breaths.

In reaction to America's financial quagmire, or because of it, the union of Russia and China created a global empire with a ten-million-man army, natural resources, the world's largest gold holdings, and a population eager to reclaim national greatness. The new nation was called Hsia. The name was a tribute to the Mongol conquerors who first united these lands in the twelfth century. Some old Soviet satellite nations reluctantly rejoined the fold, having given up their misplaced confidence in NATO and the European Union. After America's withdrawal, France, Germany, and England placed their faith with the United Nations. Collapsing currencies, unmanageable current-account deficits, massive sovereign debt, and the collapse of the US dollar as the world's reserve currency plagued all countries, especially Eastern Europe.

The Hsian central bank's governor, Zhou Xiaochuan, said their goal was to create a new global reserve currency "that is disconnected from individual nations and is able to remain stable in the long run, removing deficiencies caused by using credit-based debtor currencies. The financial failures and worldwide spillover reflect the inherent vulnerabilities of the old American system." Mr. Xiaochuan's comments gave a clear critique of Hsian views of the changing world order and the weakened dollar-dominated monetary system.

World order dissolved quickly in the leadership vacuum created by a crippled and retreating America. Western European countries were forced to foot the bill, propping up Eastern European nations. Eastern nations wasted billions on consumption booms and pork barrel construction projects during good times. Hungary and the three Baltic nations collapsed first. Banks in Germany, Sweden, and Austria suffered staggering losses because they invested heavily in Eastern Europe. Desperate unilateral currency controls forced loan repayments in local currency, in effect expropriating foreign bank assets. A massive wave of defaults and nationalistic protectionist instincts unraveled the European Single Market.

The European Congress of Trade Unions organized marches that filled the streets of all European capital cities. Most Europeans lost everything and now had no stake in civil order. The marches were a warning shot to governments, which pumped billions of Euros into troubled banks that failed anyway, destroying the public's confidence.

In Warsaw one hundred thousand protesters stormed government buildings and the national radio station broadcast center. Armed troops of the European Unified Forces were called in to disperse looting crowds. Tear gas and rubber bullets were ineffective. Tanks, machine guns, and urban battle tactics were effective. Every European capital city was in flames.

Global financial market gyrations pushed Ireland, Greece, and Spain into a financial black hole, followed by the western Balkans and

Turkey. The European Central Bank, European Bank of Reconstruction and Development, the European Investment Bank, and the International Monetary Fund failed under scandalous disorganization and chaos. The Czech Republic and Estonia joined together, creating a desperate bailout fund that was quickly exhausted. Eastern European citizens felt they had been deserted by the West. Hsia was eager to reassert influence in the area.

With few exceptions, the US Navy remained in port, as much from a lack of fuel and supplies as a lack of will. Two US carrier groups operated in the Mediterranean. A shortage of fuel and supplies required alternation between each group. When the *Lincoln* arrived at port, fuel, supplies, and armaments were offloaded onto the waiting *Texas Group*. There were not enough naval resources available to operate two carriers simultaneously in any single operational theater.

France and Germany faced three thousand modern Hsiaian tanks and two hundred well-equipped infantry divisions on their eastern frontier. The European armies had worn-out, obsolete 1990s-era US surplus equipment acquired after American disarmament. When France objected to Hsiaian naval aggression in the Mediterranean, Hsia cut off winter natural gas supplies, and five thousand French citizens froze to death. Closing the Canadian border, the American government anticipated a French capitulation in Europe, causing Quebec to join Hsia. That created an uncontrollable situation to the north. Alaska was abandoned and alone.

Arab nations unified under a secret security agreement written by Hsia after assurances that Israel could be carved up like a ripe melon. The treaty language protecting Jewish citizens was negotiated with the dovish Israeli government in exchange for Israeli nuclear disarmament commitments. The deal dissolved in blood once Hsia stopped protecting the Jewish refugee camps and the United Arab flag was raised over Tel Aviv. The slaughter and rape of the defenseless Jewish population was not carried on American television. "It would promote unfair negative stereotype views of peaceful Arab nations," the networks said.

OPEC joined with Hsia, creating the World Energy Council. Submissive nations purchased oil at wellhead costs. Others were forced to pay confiscatory amounts, leading to hyperinflation, more civil unrest, and anarchy around the world. Hsia replaced the old International Monetary Fund (IMF) and Floating Exchange System with a gold-based economy controlled by the Russian Central Bank. Russia and China demanded payment in gold for the US Treasury bills and notes they held. The US was stripped of its remaining gold reserves. The dollar was worthless on world exchange markets. It purchased what ten cents did just eight months earlier. The government was spending more this year than in all previous years combined. Economic freedom was now in question as government printing presses run full time and the economy fell further into chaos.

America's traditional abundance had turned into desperation. Formerly well-stocked grocery shelves were now empty. The hungry waited hours for the chance to buy a small loaf of bread or sausage links from government stores. Most often they received worthless rain checks when daily supplies ran out. In large American cities food was delivered on heavily guarded trucks with armed soldiers riding in the back and front. In Boston, flour arrived by ship and was offloaded onto enclosed tractor-trailers with special water cannon platforms attached to the front and rear. Another guard was positioned on top.

Tear-gas canisters were fired to disperse starving crowds each time the electric dock gates opened. Some in the crowds lifted terribly thin children with protruding stomachs. "We need help, please feed our children!" They held small plastic containers like those originally used for cream cheese or spreadable butter, hoping that a sack of flour would fall from the trucks or a sympathetic guard would toss one onto the street. Thousands lined each side of the road, closing in tighter and tighter as the food trucks approached. Crouched behind protective platforms, front and rear guards aimed water cannons and stood at the ready. Each city block or so, the guard on top tossed a flour sack into the crowd. The distraction allowed the truck to proceed as the desperate and hungry fought for food like starving animals.

South and Central America, including Mexico, formed the Latin American Defense Organization, LADO. Illegal immigration created imbalances in the southwestern United States, and when the Hispanic governors of New Mexico and Arizona requested honorary LADO membership, the federal US government was powerless to stop it. Remaining US military installations in these areas were placed on alert as South American LADO armored divisions moved north, threatening US border towns.

LADO insurgents in Southern California and parts of Texas encouraged bloody street fighting and terrorism in San Diego, Dallas, and Phoenix. The Mexican president accused the US of genocide, demanding a return to the pre-1848 borders. A claim backed by LADO and Hsia and the World Court they now controlled.

Neglect and mismanagement had taken a terrible toll on the American Air Force as well. Officers regularly called fighter squadrons, ordered jets scrambled, and measured combat readiness. One New Mexico base in question was expected to have twenty combat-ready F18s but could scramble only ten on short notice. Of the ten flyable fighters, ten were successfully scrambled—by Air Force accounting, that equaled one hundred percent combat ready. The Pentagon reported one hundred percent readiness for a base with fifty percent of its fighters grounded. The inoperable jets were used as donors for increasingly hard to find spare parts. When waves of LADO MIG fighters threatened US southwestern airspace in swarms like angry hornets, they faced only token resistance from a dispirited US Air Force.

17

THE NEW AMERICAN PRESIDENT WAS elected on an appeasement platform promising disarmament and more jobs in exchange for peace accords with Hsia and LADO. She carried the election with a sixty-five percent landslide victory, the largest in American history. This State of the Union Address would be the first for the new administration.

Washington DC had the feel of a police state as the presidential limousine, under heavy guard, made its way down Pennsylvania Avenue to the Capitol Building. President Sanders admired the stern-looking soldiers manning mobile water cannons. Originally designed to fight fires in high-rise buildings, these vehicles proved more effective at dispersing disorderly crowds. When aimed at protesters, high-pressure water from the roof-mounted water cannons broke arms, legs, and ribs. Steel grates welded on their fronts, similar to "cow guards" found on old steam locomotives, allowed the vehicles to maneuver freely in large crowds.

The president made one final call as her heavily armored limousine neared the Capitol. "Everything is set. I don't anticipate anything we are not able to handle and handle quickly. We have a deal." She placed the satellite phone back in its cradle. The premier of Hsia smiled as the phone conversation ended; he was pleased the young US president was so agreeable.

Desmond was the last to leave the office this evening. He shut down the computers, locked the doors, and waited alone in cold rain at the bus stop. He lived in a prosperous suburban neighborhood of fine homes, large lots, and double garages. Recently most of his neighbors' homes had been foreclosed. Once the banks failed, the neighbors moved back as squatters. Americans in the 1930s were better off. Desmond exited the bus, buttoned his overcoat tight against the evening chill, and walked the two blocks home. His solitude was interrupted by the distant sound of a small airplane. "Unusual on such an overcast evening," he whispered to himself. Desmond looked up for a moment, saw nothing, and continued on. He opened the front gate and went inside.

"You must be freezing. How was your day?" Karen and Isabella were anticipating his arrival with a dinner of red beans with rice and a warm fire in the living room. Desmond reached down to pet Prince, a mutt he'd had for many years. He was named for another dog Desmond loved as a boy. Prince was old now, with shedding hair and arthritic back legs. Desmond pet his old friend, unconcerned by the pet hair on the rug. "Warm up by the fire. I'll finish preparing dinner," Karen said.

Karen's family was originally from Spain but settled in Texas during the late 1600s. They moved to New Orleans in the 1930s, looking for work. "Are we going to be okay?" Karen asked.

"Yes, of course. Haven't we always," Desmond said unconvincingly, trying to disguise doubt. He finished dinner and kissed Karen on the forehead.

"The president's speech is starting, hurry!" Isabella said from the living room.

President Sanders entered the Senate chambers. "Mr. Speaker, the president of the United States!"

It seemed to take forever as the president made her way toward the podium. She stopped to shake everyone's hand along the aisle. Most senators and congressmen were enthusiastic party members supporting the new president. "Thank you, thank you, please, please," she said. After a few more minutes the president began, looking at party supporters, then back at the teleprompter. First she covered routine items and listed the accomplishments of her young administration. "We seek new powers that guarantee economic liberty, not threaten it!" She allowed applause to continue for a while. "Identifying new punishments for anti-economic behavior will protect law-abiding, hardworking citizens from those with economic malice in their hearts. Economic terrorism and financial crimes against the American economy are now punishable offenses. Those suspected of these crimes can be jailed for hoarding private wealth that rightfully belongs to all American citizens," she said.

"Because of the serious nature of these offenses, we are removing the prohibition on double jeopardy. These heartless criminals can be and will be tried twice for the same offense if warranted by the evidence!" The applause rolled across the chamber floor. "For special classes of serious economic crime, we intend to eliminate the potential for error by reducing the unnecessary scope of trial by jury."

Desmond looked over at Karen and Isabella. "My god! What are they doing?" he said.

President Sanders continued. "Government security agents have identified those people who match anti-economic profiles. Closed-circuit television cameras around the country have helped monitor and track these greedy individuals. We are utilizing unmanned miniature aircraft drones that are nearly invisible from the street. They loiter and track these individuals, unseen, while sending images to nearby security agents. Lists of these economic malcontents are now public record. Every law-abiding citizen has an obligation to thoroughly review these lists," the president said. "All honest citizens are expected to help locate and arrest the accused. Once the criminal is arrested, their property will be confiscated for the benefit of the community.

"Fighting new economic threats requires new powers. We are building a financial DNA database containing records of everyone arrested in our land," the president said.

"Can they track innocent people never charged with crimes?" Karen asked.

The president continued. "Over the last year, criminals suspected of anti-American economic crimes have been secretly tracked using these new methods and will be arrested soon. IRS records, Security Services records, and bank records will be centralized to develop a comprehensive database recording the financial DNA of every economic criminal in the country." The intentional pause encouraged more applause.

"Government has maintained its end of a most important bargain. We have not interfered with the operation or establishment of organized religion. We have never interfered even when important political policies were repeatedly attacked from the pulpit. Government has honored commitments under the separation provisions, even when religion was exploited as a massive tax dodge by charlatans," the president said.

"While government has behaved responsibly, churches have not. We have stayed out of religion; they have not stayed out of politics. All churches now face annual permitting requirements and retroactive tax penalties for those determined to have engaged in disruptive politics. Confiscated religious buildings will be turned over to local government for the public good."

"No one can outlaw our thoughts. Our minds are fortresses that are always free," Desmond said to Karen and Isabella. "Don't worry. Everything will be fine," he assured them.

Foreign corporations built factories and plants around the country. Strong foreign currencies made investing in America very lucrative, but salaries for American workers were paid in worthless dollars. An annual income of five hundred thousand dollars could hardly feed a family and pay rent.

"We need more foreign investment, more manufacturing, more production, and more exports. The American workforce must become more productive," the president continued. "We must work tirelessly to rebuild our economy. We must work harder than any other nation. We must keep foreign investment here and export more. Economic survival depends on this."

Congressmen and senators were on their feet, cheering.

"Production quotas must not be missed, especially for our most important exports, like biofuel. The eight-hour workday and forty-hour week and early retirements have become unaffordable relics of the industrial revolution," the president added.

At evening's end Desmond believed the American people were being led into slavery.

"We seek new powers that guarantee economic liberty, not threaten it!" President Sanders concluded.

Desmond had felt heartbreaking loss once before, after Hurricane Katrina destroyed New Orleans. The soul of his beloved city perished when the levees broke. Desmond wept. He knew there was no one coming to the rescue this time.

Isabella said good night and went to bed. Desmond was happy she was too young to understand. In silence, he walked over to the TV and turned it off, uninterested in the opposition's response. "Useless," he mumbled. He pet Prince gently on the head. "Sleep well, old friend," and he headed to bed.

After years of marriage, Karen never had seen him this way. During all of life's ups and downs, triumphs and losses, Desmond remained optimistic by nature, but not now. He always knew the rules, believing that work, perseverance, and creativity would win out. Now success was a punishable offense.

18

KAREN AND DESMOND ALWAYS READ before falling asleep. Sometimes after a long day, he would get through only one or two paragraphs before his eyelids became too heavy. Other times he could read a hundred pages. Desmond enjoyed nonfiction, especially economic history or military history. But lately he had been reading a fantasy series about treasure hunters in the Florida Keys, and he relished the temporary escape.

Desmond opened the book, then placed it on his chest. He was content to stare at the ceiling. Karen leaned over and gave him a quick kiss—the type shared by lovers who have grown comfortable over years of familiarity. "Try to get some sleep. Things will look better in the morning. They always do," she reassured him. Desmond fell asleep, woke an hour or two later, walked to the kitchen for a glass of water, turned off the reading light, and tried to fall back asleep.

Prince was restless. He growled and barked for no apparent reason. "Go to sleep, Prince," Desmond said, accepting the fact that he would not get much shut-eye this night. He heard something outside near the front porch that upset Prince. *Neighborhood cats,* Desmond thought. He dismissed the hushed voices he thought he heard outside as illusionary tricks played by his exhausted mind. Until the kitchen door was kicked in. A moment later the front door was torn from its hinges.

Neighbors armed with baseball bats, hammers, axes, and crowbars smashed windows and walls. They stormed into the bedroom, pulling Karen and Desmond apart. "You are on the president's list. Desmond Dupree, you have committed economic crimes against the American people!" the mob leader said as he held a serrated fish-cleaning knife to Desmond's throat. He was wearing a black knitted mask over his face and a sleeveless shirt exposing a Liberty Bell tattoo on his left shoulder. Desmond knew this man. It was Beer Boy! Beer Boy had given Desmond's name to government authorities in exchange for the promise of a government job. He was happy to drive from Baton Rouge to participate in the arrest because he was deeply jealous of Desmond's financial success.

The mob ripped apart walls, shredded the upholstered furniture, and pulled up floorboards. Whatever was not destroyed was tossed to wives waiting outside. Desmond saw Prince still trying to defend his home as he was pummeled again and again with bats and hammers. "*Passio Christi, conforta me,*" Desmond said to himself, renewing his strength. "Go ahead, cut my throat. You don't have the guts to do it!" he said to Beer Boy.

"It doesn't matter, the federal security agents will be here in a minute!" Beer Boy replied with a smartass smirk on his face.

Desmond was not the only victim arrested this dark night. The local authorities were rounding up everyone on the president's list. Escorted by black Hummers, they used rental moving trucks to transport the detainees. Unmanned surveillance drones relayed the scene to security officers in undisclosed locations. They had heavy equipment ready to rip homes apart if gold or cash was not found easily.

The convoy rode through the night making many stops. Desmond's arrest was next. Neighborhood women spit on him as he was dragged from the house. He was thrown into the truck by muscular men with covered faces. He reached out to Karen and Isabella but was pulled away. The truck doors were closed and locked. Desmond heard a bulldozer engine starting up, preparing to demolish everything in search of hidden valuables. The truck was nearly full, each prisoner telling a similar story. Desmond did not know if he would ever see Karen and Isabella again.

There were no windows or seats. Captives were packed into the truck like the three hundred French soldiers trapped by the Viet Minh at Dien Bien Phu. The convoy drove for a long time, making many turns and stops along the way. Conversation died down as the hopelessness of the situation settled upon the thoughts of the unfortunate prisoners. Some wept for their families. Some wanted to escape. Some planned confessions. Most were silent.

Desmond grew up poor in the Ninth Ward area of New Orleans. There was nothing material they could take from him that he had not already done without. But he was devastated because he was unable to protect Karen and Isabella. Thoughts of what he could or should have done ran over and over in his head, haunting him. Death this night, defending his home and family, that was what Desmond now wished for, but the time had passed. He hoped Karen remembered the survival plan he prepared for her.

Desmond admired the courage of soldiers, especially those who faced certain death with honor. He found inspiration in the words of a Confederate officer killed on the battlefield: "Tell my father I died with my face to the enemy." Devastation turned to rage. Desmond's concern for his family was all-consuming. He would never leave them unprotected again. He would never be dragged from his home and spit upon again. He was not yet ready to give up, not before he finished this and not before Beer Boy begged for his life on hands and knees. For now faith and courage were all Desmond had.

The vigilantes ransacked the Dupree home. Satisfied with Desmond's imprisonment, they moved on to the next target. Among the rubble that had recently been their comfortable home, Karen waited, sitting on the front steps with Isabella. When she was certain everyone had gone, she found the hot water heater lying on its side, leaking. Karen unscrewed the thin metal covering as Desmond had told her to do. Hidden inside the tank's insulation were dozens and dozens of gold coins, many hundred-dollar bills, and a .45 semiautomatic pistol. Desmond had left a short note. "You know what to do. This will help get you and Isabella to Texas. Stay with family. I love you."

19

WORD OF THE LATE-NIGHT arrests was greeted mostly with celebration and support. President Sanders' popularity ratings were up nearly fifteen points, a strong majority believing that the country was now heading in the "correct" direction. The president called a noon press conference to address the American people on the successful outcome. "We have scored a significant achievement. Economic malcontents across our land were rounded up. Today, America is a better place!" she said.

Not everyone agreed. Alaska became a refuge for fleeing business owners, doctors, lawyers, and the American professional class now under assault. President Sanders said, "These people created a heads-I-win-tails-you-lose capitalism. They got rich by speculating with our money. When everything fell apart the taxpayers got the bill. They can flee with the clothes on their backs. We keep everything else. Let them go!" Canadian authorities allowed American refugees to cross the border without passports.

On the American side of the Washington State border, guards stole everything of value. Cars were confiscated; rape was common and used as a political weapon. Families were separated. Heavily armed Canadian forces maintained defensive positions one hundred yards from the American side of the border. Combat-trained Canadian Special Forces were shocked by the inhumanity they witnessed. They were eager to enter the fight but were unable to interfere unless they were fired upon first. The Canadians also provided emergency medical aid and a fleet of ambulances to carry the seriously ill and injured to Vancouver hospitals.

Some American refugees tried to cross the Canadian border at remote northwest locations. American helicopters and jets made that a risky gamble. Desmond was a political prisoner in his own country because they believed he had money. Yet the most effective way to guarantee safe passage into Canada was to bribe American Border Guards with gold coins. The hypocrisy was inescapable.

President Sanders did nothing to stop the suffering. She encouraged it. It was like the Cuban boat lift of the late 1970s in reverse. Castro used the opportunity to rid himself of troublemakers, dissidents, and nonbelievers. He emptied Cuba's prisons and psychiatric hospitals and sent most of his problems to South Florida. A naïve President Carter was waiting with open arms. President Sanders believed she was using Alaska in a similar fashion, a convenient way to cleanse society of America's new class of "economic untouchables." It was like America's Siberia, except these Americans were not defenseless victims. Alaska was still a land of rugged individualism. Perhaps it was the last such place. The president miscalculated.

Alaska continued oil and gas exploration and production despite congressional restrictions. Hsia (ignoring global-warming fears) was always willing and eager to purchase Alaskan petroleum.

Through directional drilling techniques off the coast and in international waters, Hsia was able to steal more Alaskan oil than it purchased. Long, directional drill lines reached into Alaskan oil fields from numerous Hsian rigs in the Bering and Beaufort seas. They sucked Alaska's oil like giant mechanical leeches. Hsian Sukhoi fighter jets flew patrols just off the coast, attempting to intimidate Alaskan forces. During the Cold War, Soviet Bear-H bombers flew up to US airspace and turned, testing the resolve and readiness of American defenses. This was the same playbook.

Alaska used oil revenue to support the new refugees, providing shelter and food. The cash also purchased state-of-the-art arms. The

Alaskan National Guard became an efficient, well-equipped, all-weather fighting force. Only Finland, Norway, and Hsia had similar forces capable of conducting operations in extreme winter conditions. The old National Guard units evolved into the Alaskan Defense Forces (ADF). If ranked independently the ADF would be the world's sixth largest standing army.

20

THE F22 RAPTOR WAS THE fifth and final generation of American fighter aircraft. Original Department of Defense intentions were to purchase 339 at a unit cost of 137 million each. After congressional budget cutbacks, the final procurement was a tally of only twenty aircraft. The cost per aircraft would have been much lower had Congress not discontinued the program. Thus the entire sixty-five-billion-dollar developmental costs or "sunk costs" were divided by the number of fighters actually built. Congressional cuts made the Raptor the most expensive aircraft aloft. It was more costly than the Cold War-era B-2 Stealth Bomber. The Chairman of the House Finance Services Committee said when he proposed cutting F22 funding, "We are building an airplane that is designed to defeat the Soviet Union. I think we can save these billions." He saved nothing.

The F22 Stealth Raptor was by far the most capable fighter ever produced. It easily outperformed other jets like the Sukhoi fighters from Russia and now Hsia. Using two Pratt & Whitney F-PW-100 turbofan engines, it was capable of reaching a maximum speed of Mach 2.34. Raptors carried air-to-air missiles in internal weapon bays, a twenty-millimeter Vulcan rotary cannon, six AIM-9 Sidewinder missiles, and four Sparrow missiles. Three F22s had been stationed at the Fort Worth Joint Reserve Base in Texas. They were moved north to prevent the possibility of falling into LADO hands or the hands of a breakaway Texas Republic.

US Air Force Colonel Wayne Parsons was a veteran of Desert Shield, Desert Storm, and the second Iraq war. He had nearly four thousand combat hours flying F18s and later F22 Raptors. He was the son of a Vietnam-era F4 Fathom pilot and a Thai mother once employed by the American embassy. Colonel Parsons considered political views to be a private, personal matter and seldom discussed controversial issues. "I take orders from civilian-elected officials. It is not my job to question," he had said repeatedly. Secretly he harbored deep personal inner conflict.

His wife, Vickie, had been an executive with a major Wall Street investment bank. She worked her way up from a junior assistant position to senior analyst. She was responsible for nearly one-third of her firm's annual revenues. Vickie held three degrees from respected universities and numerous investment banking licenses and credentials.

Her firm was one of the first to be nationalized by President Sanders. Mrs. Parsons' office files were confiscated, including her computer hard drive. Federal agents returned a few days later and placed her under arrest without filing any specific charges. Colonel Parsons learned from friends at the Pentagon that his wife was being held at a maximum security federal facility in Louisiana. He swore an oath to "protect and defend the Constitution of the United States"— not to this current administration ripping it apart.

Routine northern border patrol flights between Saskatchewan and Montana were used to locate and track "Claim Jumpers." The Jumpers were Americans illegally attempting to cross the Canadian border. The three F22 Raptors crossed northern US terrain at high-speed, low-altitude flights using Active Electronically Scanned Array systems. Reporting back to search and hunt units on the ground, they tracked dozens of Claim Jumper groups simultaneously. Colonel Parsons knew the unfortunate fate waiting for those he helped hunt down. That was not his problem. "The rapes, murders, and robberies are collateral damage and thus unavoidable," he tried unsuccessfully to convince himself.

Thus far, this night's mission, code-named "Eagle View," had been uneventful. Two groups of Claim Jumpers on foot were detected and easily tracked down by Army ground units in Hummers following coordinates provided by Colonel Parsons' jet fighters. Another group of five vehicles were detected racing north fast. They were cut off just south of the Canadian border near Regina. The colonel issued standing orders returning to base after another successful patrol. The three F22s crossed into Washington State airspace from Montana on schedule as expected. They headed for the Sixty-fifth Fighter Wing base near Olympia.

On cue, each flight computer was manually overridden by the pilots awaiting additional orders from Colonel Parsons. What he was about to do was the best way to honor his solemn pledge to defend the Constitution and avenge his wife. As planned, he issued bearings for a due north turn. "On my mark, three, two, one—commence turn now," he said calmly.

"Eagle View. This is Olympia Base air traffic control. Northern heading is unauthorized. Return to previous heading." The controller said a moment later, with no emotion, "Return to previous heading or you will be shot down." The three F22s crossed into Canadian airspace, traveling over Mach two at treetop level.

"This is Eagle View. Border patrol flight from the Sixty-fifth Fighter Wing defecting to the Alaskan Defense Forces. Seeking peaceful passage to Alaskan airspace," Colonel Parsons announced to Canadian Defense Command over special emergency channels. "Please assist, urgent," he repeated. "Detect multiple armed US fighters in pursuit."

The days when the US could push Canada around had long since passed. "Eagle View, this is Canadian Defense Command. We are tracking three groups of F18s on your tail." The controller issued a series of maneuvers, leading Eagle View closer to Canadian defenses and springing a deadly trap upon the older F18s. "Come on in, little brother. We'll close the door behind you," the Canadian controller said.

The Canadian Defense Command had secretly acquired Surface-Launched Medium-Range Air Defense Systems (SL-AMRAAM) from India, which acquired the systems from Raytheon and Kongsberg defense contractors. "Eagle View, the trap is set. Deliver the prey." Colonel Parsons' F22s screamed past in full afterburners, at an altitude of two hundred feet. The earth trembled beneath. The first group of F18s flew directly over hidden Canadian SL-AMRAAM mobile launchers a moment later.

Each launcher mounted six missiles on a turret that provided 360-degree coverage. The Canadian Battle Management Command used advanced target range radar to carry out target acquisition. Once this radar locked on, the kill probability was ninety-eight percent. The four-meter-long high-velocity missiles traveled at Mach four and had high agility to counter-evasive maneuvers. The first two F18s disappeared from radar. The third dropped more altitude in a desperate attempt to avoid similar destruction, but the missile's guidance system was already locked on like a dog in heat. It slammed the fighter just behind the cockpit, splitting the F18 in half as it somersaulted into the forest below.

Colonel Parsons circled around, gaining position behind the other F18 group. He glanced at Vickie's photo taped to the cockpit monitor. "This is for you, baby!" he said. The F22's stealth capabilities assured invisibility. He opened the trapdoor on the right wing, exposing the Vulcan rotary cannon. His F22 carried only 480 rounds, enough ammunition for five seconds of sustained fire. It was more than he would need. Colonel Parsons preferred using the cannon in dogfights because it made the kill shot more personal. He locked on. "Knock-knock, motherfucker!" Another F18 disappeared in a ball of fire. The others disengaged and headed home. President Sanders denied any of this took place.

21

DESMOND SPENT MONTHS IN A small, overcrowded Florida county jail. He tried to keep track of the days, but this proved to be nearly impossible. Every day was exactly like every other. There was nothing to distinguish Monday from Thursday or Sunday for that matter. He did notice a mild change of the seasons as the humidity of the Florida panhandle decreased, signaling an early fall. His cement cell cooled slightly.

Desmond inquired again and again, "What am I charged with? You can't hold me like this forever. What are the charges?"

"You will have your answer soon. Very soon. Perhaps we should just farm you out!" the prison guard said with a laugh, repeating the phrase. "Farmed out!" Desmond could accept his fate if only he knew what it was. He could not accept this constant unknown. Mental confinement was more painful than any physical prison he could face. *What is this stupid guard talking about, "farmed out"?* he wondered.

At sunrise four old school buses—repainted white and escorted, like bookends, by army trucks with flashing blue lights—appeared. Arriving in a cloud of dust, the convoy turned off the main highway onto the two-mile dirt road leading to the isolated prison. The "Walton County Public Schools" sign on each bus was painted over and replaced with two words: Federal Prisoners. As the buses got closer, Desmond noticed unusual modifications. Iron reinforcement rods were haphazardly welded across the windows along the entire length of each bus. All glass was removed. Desmond wondered what would happen to anyone trapped inside in the event of an accident or fire. The driver sat behind a reinforced cage with a shotgun mount. The first row of seats was reversed so that guards could keep a constant eye on prisoners. "This is not good," Desmond said to the man standing next to him.

The routine was different this day. Prisoners did not return to their cells after roll call as usual. They were ordered to remain standing, anticipating instructions to board the buses. "*Passio Christi, conforta me,*" Desmond said. The prisoner standing to his right looked over and said, "Your Latin god is not much help now, I'm afraid." The buses were loaded quickly with about sixty prisoners each. They sat two to a seat, side by side, handcuffed to reinforced frames. Soldiers positioned themselves at the front of each bus, weapons loaded and ready. Their serious nature indicated that they had done this many times before and would not tolerate trouble. The prisoners boarded the buses with nothing except the clothes on their backs and a peanut butter sandwich. The convoy reached the main highway, turned right, and headed west.

Desmond's favorite aunt lived in Atlanta. In 1976, he rode with his dad in the family's Chevy Impala station wagon to Atlanta for a visit. Desmond loved this time together with his dad. They talked about everything from girls to politics to music. The station wagon did not have air-conditioning. Desmond loved riding with the windows down. He enjoyed the breeze in his hair and moving his hand against the wind's resistance like a windsurfer. The open windows of the prison bus brought back these memories. He was still free in his mind. Desmond closed his eyes and smiled. The bus rolled down I-10 with the wind in his hair.

The interstate was nearly deserted. Where were the over-the-road commercial trucks? In three hours he had counted only two. If there were more, they would have nowhere to buy fuel anyway. Nearly every station was boarded up and closed. Some appeared to have been taken over by vagrants living in abandoned cars. There was no shortage of military activity however. Long convoys heading both east and west were common. After a few hours Desmond's convoy reached a Biloxi exit. A tan-painted army fuel tanker waited under heavy guard. The refueling process for the six vehicles in Desmond's convoy took nearly forty-five minutes. Heat built up quickly in the stationary buses sitting idle in the midday Mississippi sun.

The convoy rolled into Slidell and continued north on I-12, heading toward Baton Rouge. They crossed the Mississippi River at Baton Rouge on the old Highway 90 bridge and headed in the direction of New Roads. The bridge was built by Governor Huey Long in the 1930s. It was exactly the same design as the one built in New Orleans connecting Avondale and Metairie. Car lanes were on each side with double train tracks down the middle. Huey said that Louisiana's roads and bridges were so bad that the weather could not cross the state. He set out to change that. A military freight train was crossing from the opposite direction as Desmond's bus approached. The vibration was unsettling and could not be safe. No one worried about bridge inspections and other such things anymore.

Desmond was first to realize where the convoy was heading. "My god! The farm! They are bringing us to the farm!" he said. Now Desmond understood what the wise-cracking guard in Florida meant when he said they would be "farmed out." The main gate resembled a toll booth on a major interstate like the New Jersey Turnpike. Six lanes entered under a semicircle arch, where each vehicle was searched.

Guards with dogs rolled mirrors on long sticks under cars and buses, searching the underside of all incoming traffic. The entire front gate area was brightly lit by floodlights powered by large biofuel-driven generators. Eighteen thousand acres of the world's richest farm land, with the Mississippi River circling around three sides, created the perfect location for the country's last and most notorious working plantation prison.

"I know this place!" Desmond said. "I know this place. It's nicknamed the Farm. This is Angola. Louisiana's state prison!"

22

ANGOLA'S FERTILE SOIL WAS FAMOUS for growing almost everything: sweet potatoes, cotton, soy beans, or sugarcane. It was also known for the hopeless desperation of the unfortunate men condemned to die there. Cotton had been Angola's most common crop for the last hundred years. During that time smaller plots were set aside to grow food for the prison kitchen. Angola was a self-sufficient enterprise for most of its history. Prisoners, after working in the large fields for fourteen hours, were then required to spend two hours cultivating the smaller plots. Prison guards stole the best produce, sold it, and split the cash with their supervisors, leaving little for prisoners to eat.

The national economic collapse ushered in many changes. Fourteen thousand acres were now used to grow sugarcane, for biofuel production. In ideal summer conditions, cane grew thirteen inches per week. It was more economical than corn-based biofuels. The cane was refined into fuel at the world's largest biofuel refinery, built on the northeast corner of Angola's property along the Mississippi River. Sugarcane was grown and refined into biofuel in an efficient process operated by prison slave labor. Thus Angola was the world's largest producer of biofuel, making the prison an important, heavily guarded strategic asset.

"Get up, you fuckers!" guards yelled as Desmond's bus pulled past the front gates. "You're home, boys," they said. Dressed in riot gear, guards rode on horseback along the sides of the bus, dragging their batons over the steel rods covering the bus windows. Clack, clack, clack, clack—it was a frightening sound. "This place is like Hotel California," the guard standing at the front of the bus explained. "You can check out. But you can never leave!" He pointed to a plot of land lined with freshly dug trenches organized in parallel rows. "That's where we bury dumb bastards that try to escape or just piss us off," he said while cocking his shotgun with an up-and-down motion.

Desmond assumed all this drama was calculated to frighten new arrivals into compliance, like army boot camp. The guard reached over and unlocked the handcuffs of an overweight prisoner sitting in the first seat to the right. "Fat prisoners are useless. Get out of here! Run!" he demanded.

"No please, I don't want to run away! Please!" the prisoner pleaded. The guard put the shotgun barrel against the crying prisoner's forehead as he began counting backward from ten, nine, eight... "Move, you fat fuck!"

Running for his life, the desperate prisoner made it only twenty feet before he was shot in the back. The impact of the shotgun blast thrust him forward another five feet before his lifeless body collapsed facedown. "This should be a teaching moment for you other treasonous bastards. Don't try to escape," the guard said, laughing about the short distance the fat man ran. His lifeless body was dragged feet first by two horseback-mounted guards and dropped into a freshly dug trench.

"That was some funny shit. Did you see that fat boy try to run?" Desmond could hear the cavalier conversations of two nearby guards.

Desmond was chained together with others and marched into an industrial metal building. They were led to wooden cots stacked three high and arranged close together in long rows. Each prisoner was issued brown pants and a brown shirt with "ASP," Angola State Penitentiary, stenciled across the back. On each wooden cot was a single gray cotton blanket, no pillow. The structures supporting the cots were designed with a slot at each end so that prisoners could remain chained together even while sleeping. Desmond could not sleep.

The day started at 4 a.m. "Heave to. Hit the deck." A guard armed with a wooden club barked orders while clubbing the feet of anyone slow to move. For breakfast, prisoners were marched single file past large metal tubs containing "sugartack," made from the gray mushy byproduct of sugarcane processing, shaped into five-inch patties and left to dry. The patties resembled pancakes but had no taste or nutritional value. Each prisoner was allowed two sugartack patties and one cup of water, obtained from a cistern using cups secured by rope.

Desmond took one bite and tossed his sugartack patty to the ground where others had done the same thing. "You'll get used to it," a guard said. "Everyone eventually does." Desmond had always loved breakfast, especially on Sunday. Karen had a wonderful recipe for coffee cake that took about twenty minutes to bake. Meanwhile, Desmond prepared café au lait. A local radio station played contemporary jazz while Desmond and Karen spent lazy Sunday mornings enjoying each other's company.

As the sun began to rise, Desmond and his fellow prisoners were lined up and marched out to the sugarcane fields. They met another group of prisoners heading back in their direction. Some had no shoes, ripped clothing, and cuts and bruises. All were covered with a filthy black dust. Many were missing teeth. All were malnourished.

"How long have you guys been here?" Desmond asked in a very low voice as the columns passed each other.

"Two months."

"One week."

"Four weeks." Each man quietly answered Desmond's question as they moved past. "Can't remember," one man said.

"Stay out of the fire rooms. Worse than hell!" another warned.

The last man in line looked familiar to Desmond. He was frail and held his head down. "Dr. Sonny?" Desmond called out. "Sonny?"

Sonny kept his head down and did not acknowledge Desmond as he moved past.

The man behind Desmond explained that he had lived in California years before. "In the desert they have wasps that are four inches long with one-inch stingers. They lay one larva in a hole. The wasp then stings a tarantula, paralyzing it. It drags the spider into the hole, where the larva feeds on it. The spider's organs are eaten last, keeping it alive and fresh as long as possible. We are the tarantula and government is the wasp. They will keep us alive as long as we're useful."

The Angola biofuel plant had been built quickly. No attention was paid to either environmental issues or safety. Its location on the banks of the Mississippi River was ideal for receiving coal shipments used to operate the refining process. Coal barges were unloaded and the coal stacked on docks. Prisoners used wheelbarrows to move the coal to chutes that led to storage bunkers. Other prisoners worked in the bunkers as coal rattled down the chutes. They used shovels to spread the coal evenly as it filled storage rooms. Exhausted prisoners who collapsed were quickly buried alive.

The primitive biofuel refining process required massive distilling furnaces fueled by "fire rooms." These were the "man killers" Desmond heard about. Heat was needed to power the cracking units necessary for the biofuel refining process. The fire rooms were beastly hot, like an inferno. There were twenty fire rooms with five firebox doors each. Prisoners stripped to their underwear, shoveling coal as the guards demanded, "More fire! More fire!" Ten prisoners worked each firebox, shoveling coal from the bunkers into fire rooms. Guards clubbed anyone working below expectations. "More fire. More fire!"

In order to heat efficiently, coal had to be spread evenly over the furnace grates as it burned. One prisoner at each firebox handled the slice bar, a piece of steel about twelve feet long with a flat end-hook. The bar was used as a coal-spreading tool, allowing more air into the fire and increasing heat. But the fireboxes were nearly twenty feet deep, requiring slice bar operators to reach deep into the flaming infernos. Their life expectancy was less than two weeks, killed by suffocation as inhaled burning embers scorched their lungs. Their final days were a hellish drowning sensation as damaged lungs took in less and less oxygen. Upon their death, other prisoners stripped the unfortunate bodies of everything useful. Clothes and shoes were used as barter in exchange for other necessities like snake meat or cigarettes. Names were quickly forgotten.

Every other day one fire room was shut down on a rotating schedule. The coal-burning process produced a byproduct called clinkers. The clinkers had to be removed and the furnace grates cleaned on a regular basis. Prisoners, covering mouths with their arms, used hoes to rake them out of the furnace onto floor plates. Others cooled the clinkers with hoses. The steam mixed with coal dust created a black residue that penetrated eyes, hair, ears, and skin crevices. The coal waste was shoveled into a chute that led directly to the Mississippi River, where the currents carried it away.

Desmond and the other prisoners approached the colossal biofuel plant for the first time. The sky was black from smoke pumped out of the ten towering stacks. Each stack was taller than the Washington Monument. The massive scale of the plant was beyond description, stretching for at least a mile. It was the world's largest "poured in place" concrete-reinforced structure. It was larger than the Hoover Dam and believed by many to be indestructible. The pollution burned Desmond's lungs. He knew he would not last long working in the plant. Years as a banker had left him unprepared for extreme physical labor. He had hoped his white-collar background would qualify him for more appropriate responsibilities. The selection process was not that precise.

Prisoners lined up single file and walked between groups of guards stationed on each side. Desmond was near the end. "*Passio Christi, conforta me,*" he repeated to himself, lips barely moving.

"Speed up, motherfuckers!" guards demanded, jabbing clubs into prisoners' kidneys, pushing them along in the process.

The first guard reached under each prisoner's shirt, feeling chest and arms. "Coal!" he said like bidding at a slave auction. "Cane, coal, coal!" he repeated while moving down the line. Physical strength determined work assignments. The strongest went to work coal, while the others went to the cane fields. Desmond was inspected. "Cane!"

23

THE HSIAN FOREIGN MINISTER DEMANDED
that Alaska be returned to Russia. "Alaska was never purchased. The
lease agreements of 1867 were valid for only one hundred years.
Alaska is now and will always be the rightful property of the Hsian
people," he said in a petition filed with the World International
Court. During the WWII Lend-Lease program, American fighter
planes were flown to Nome from Fairbanks. Soviet pilots then flew
them over the North Pole into Russia for use fighting Germans. A
number of isolated bases were established along this northern flight
path to accommodate the short-range fighters of the day. Recently,
Hsian forces had reactivated these airfields for operations against the
Alaskan Defense Forces. Bear-H bombers regularly encroached into
Alaskan airspace from the north, causing panic.

The Hsian bomber crews were relaxed as they headed toward
Alaskan airspace. Protected by a Sukhoi fighter jet, they joked about
how easy it was to violate the territory of a defenseless nation. "Are
Alaskan women this easy?" they wondered aloud and joked about
Eskimo pussy being "hot!" The two bombers flew at thirty thousand
feet. Invisible to the Hsian intruders, Colonel Parsons and the three
stealth F-22s tracked them from forty thousand feet. The F-22s, now
painted with the image of the gray wolf, representing the independence of the Alaskan Air Defense Forces, flew above and behind their
unsuspecting prey.

The kills had to be quick and clean, avoiding any distress communications from the bombers and timed so debris fell in remote, inac-
cessible areas. Blaming malfunctioning navigation gear, Hsian
diplomats would deny the flight's provocative intentions. Alaska
would deny any knowledge, involvement, or responsibility in down-
ing the bombers. They would blame unpredictable weather and offer
to organize rescue operations, "in the spring."

The Hsian bombers continued to fly straight and level, unaware of
the F22s maneuvering into "kill shot" positions behind them. The six
o'clock area of the bandits was most vulnerable to surprise attack.
While still beyond visible range, Colonel Parsons planned the kill
using his favorite Vulcan cannons. Air-to-air missiles would risk
detection from the bomber's defensive radar. He preferred cannons
anyhow. "Up close and personal," Parsons always said with a grin. "It's
not a real dogfight unless you use guns!"

The Hsian flight crews continued to believe they were violating the
airspace of a weak, defenseless nation. They were complacent behind
the protection of their single-fighter escort. The six-barrel Vulcan cannon fired six thousand high-explosive incendiary rounds per minute.
It sounded more like a powerful high-speed drill than traditional
machine gun. Colonel Parsons said it was the "voice of Satan."

Having earned the attention of all three F22s, the Sukhoi fighter
tumbled out of the sky in a ball of fire. The bomber crew's surprised
reaction time was slow, but it made little difference. They frantically
turned their heads up and down, side to side, trying to sight their
attackers—radar showed zero contacts. "Radio, Moscow!" the flight
commander ordered in a desperate tone. It was too late. The lumber-
ing beasts were defenseless against the ghostly predators determined
to kill them. The thin aluminum bomber skin offered little protection
against the tsunami of high-explosive rounds that sliced through the
flight cabins. Bodies instantly dissolved into unrecognizable heaps of
blood and flesh. The attack took less than seven seconds.

Colonel Parsons glanced at Vickie's photo. "I'm coming for you,
baby," he said quietly.

During World War II, Canada made a significant contribution to the Allied victory. More Canadian forces were involved in the conflict than from nearly any other commonwealth nation. Canadian forces were assigned one of the most difficult objectives at Normandy beaches. Allied bomber crews often requested Canadian fighter escorts on the most dangerous missions. Canadian Royal Navy destroyers protected Atlantic convoys, and thousands of Allied wounded recovered safely in Canadian hospitals.

In recent decades, Canada had lost the stomach for conflict. It hid this weakness behind a convenient belief in multiculturalism, confusing self-defense obligations with accommodating the grievances of vicious enemies. Successive governments reallocated Canadian defense appropriations to social spending, trying to buy stability. Protected under America's cold war security blanket, the country could afford to neglect defense. Canada's once proud military was reduced to a "meals on wheels" program, rushing to the aid of disaster victims around the world but incapable of fighting. Everything changes, especially when survival is on the line. Charles Darwin did not say only the strong survive. He said those that can adapt to change quickest will win. "In the struggle for survival, the fittest win out at the expense of their rivals because they succeed in adapting themselves best."

The former Canadian prime minister based policy positions on an "Understanding Agreement" with Hsia. He claimed the agreement "guaranteed peace and prosperity for the citizens of both nations." However, the deal exchanged Canadian natural resources for security promises that eroded Canadian independence. Canada was expected to look away as Hsia continued to intimidate Free Alaska and encroach on the northern Alaskan oil fields.

The current prime minister challenged Canadians to stand and fight. "I am not asking to send our boys to fight on foreign soil thousands of miles away. I am asking Canadians to stand and fight for our homes. Fight for our way of life. Fight for our history and our children. To sacrifice in defense of one's country is a glorious honor. Freedom and independence. Sacrifice and struggle." He reminded citizens of the common heritage shared between Alaska and Canada. "We have had our disagreements from time to time, but it would be unwise for outsiders to interpret family disagreements as weakness. We will stand with a Free Alaska just as we would Ontario or Quebec." He pounded his fist on the podium as thousands cheered.

Canada was caught between a collapsing America to the south, Hsia to the north, and west and LADO forces moving up the Pacific Coast. Odds were against Canadian national survival. But like a wounded bear, Canada was not going down without a fight. A new Friendship Pact between Canada and Alaska created a formidable power with abundant resources, manpower, and determination. The motto of the new Northern Alliance, "Head North to Freedom," attracted military people from across the former commonwealth nations, Europe, and America. They defected with fighter jets, equipment, and naval assets.

Warships from the world's greatest navies arrived at Alaskan and Canadian ports, where they were welcomed as brothers-in-arms. The Northern Alliance was becoming the heir of the British Empire but welcomed anyone willing to fight. Even the French in Quebec organized four armored divisions with equipment rescued from France before capitulation. The Canadian/French forces were called the Free French Resistance, honoring the fighters who helped liberate Paris in the 1940s. With guidance from former Israeli commanders, the Northern Alliance was becoming a military superpower itching for a fight and determined to kick ass.

Sixteen bombs and missiles from Israeli's secret nuclear arsenal were smuggled into the Northern Alliance as Tel Aviv was overrun. Israeli commanders correctly calculated that a limited number of nukes were not enough to stop the Arab hordes from crushing their borders. Since America was sitting this war out, Israeli commanders retreated to Canada, protecting some nukes. They survived to fight another day.

Alaskan oil fields were open for development and exploration. More oil was discovered in six months than Saudi and Iraq combined held in reserve. The Alaskan pipelines were rerouted directly into Canada. Old US shipping terminals were closed for good. The border between Alaska and Canada was opened, allowing the flow of arms and resources.

The Canadian prime minister addressed the Northern Alliance. To his right was the Alaskan president, and behind the two leaders stood Canadian Mounties in their traditional red coats, and a company of Alaskan Special Forces in winter combat fatigues. All carried Israeli-made submachine guns, including the prime minister. "An attack upon any member of the Northern Alliance will be considered an attack upon all," the prime minister said, taking a page from old NATO treaties. Except this time he planned to back that statement with iron will. "We will not fold our tents and steal away. Nor will we wait to be attacked like sheep in a field. We will not go quietly! If any nation wishes us ill, we are ready, prepared, and determined. We will win the skirmish, the battle, the coming war! God save us all!"

24

DESMOND CONSIDERED HIMSELF LUCKY TO
work the cane. He knew he would die in the bio-plant; it was a death
sentence. Cane work was the best of bad options, easy, he believed.
He was assigned to work "seed cane." He expected to spend his time
placing seeds in shallow trenches as he leisurely moved down the
rows. He was wrong. "Line up along the edge of this field. Two feet
between each of you," the guards demanded as they rode back and
forth on horseback, dropping chains at the feet of every other prisoner.

Prisoners avoided eye contact with guards and always kept their
heads down, like submissive puppies. As the horses paced back and
forth, Desmond noticed trails of blood on the ground. The guards'
spurs were designed to demand the horse's immediate attention when
jammed into the animal's quarters. The spurs were cruel, with four
rowels, each at least one inch long and rusty. The horses' quarters and
hind legs were covered with dried blood. Fresh blood was from new
wounds as the guards demanded constant obedience from the abused
animals. The horses galloped upon demand, flanks scarred with open
sores. The prisoners were treated worse. "Pick up those cane knives.
Let's go," the lead guard demanded.

Each guard had a shotgun and holster on the right side of his saddle and a leather whip coiled around the saddle's pommel. The stir-
rups were boxed in front to prevent them from getting caught up as

the horses raced through the cane fields. Prisoners were divided into teams of two each, chained together and taught how to cut and stack seed cane. The cane knife was a type of machete with a long, curved wooden handle designed for swinging the sharp blade toward the bottom of the stalks, "like a one-armed golf swing," the guard explained.

"I thought we were planting seeds!" Desmond remarked to the prisoner he was now chained to.

"Cane stalks are the seeds. The fields are replanted every four years. You're just in time," he replied.

Since sugarcane is a hybrid, seeds produce plants that are different from the originals. Planting requires unique techniques. The best cane from the best fields is selected as seed cane. It has to be cut close to the base, carefully handled and trimmed. Every few years the fields are plowed under, and new, six-inch-deep rows are dug. The rows are three feet apart and run the length of the acreage. Seed cane is laid end to end by hand, then covered with soil. New cane grows from the old, sometimes producing two or three harvests per season depending on weather conditions. This is an efficient way to grow cane, when the process is mechanized, but at Angola labor was plentiful and cheap, and everything was done by hand with primitive tools.

Desmond knew what President Sanders meant by "controlling time and production" comments in her national speech. He did not know what day or month it was. He did not know how many hours he worked each day or how many days he had worked.

Desmond's work party was divided between cutters, stackers, and drivers. Desmond was a stacker. The cutters moved into the field first, using cane knives to cut their way toward the other side of the field. It usually took two swings to cut each stalk. But the cane knives were old and dull, requiring twice as many swings and twice as much time. The guards continued to demand that work progress on schedule, which was nearly impossible without sharp knives. The guards snapped their whips like firecrackers at workers who dared fall behind.

As the cutters moved forward, Desmond picked up the cut seed cane, trimmed the leaves, bundled the stalks together, and placed them on ox carts, where the drivers hauled it to nearby fields for planting. Cane leaves are long like reeds and can be sharp as razors if handled along the edges. Desmond's hands left bloodstains on the stalks as hundreds of tiny, painful cuts bled, but he was thankful not to be a cutter. The cutters struggled to maintain an impossible pace demanded by impatient guards. "Pop, pop, pop" was heard as whips slapped against the bare backs of slower cutters up and down the field. When a man collapsed, everyone else moved up one position. Desmond was next in line to be a cutter.

The cutter in front of Desmond was working slower and slower. It was only a matter of time before he attracted attention. The guards called this "gaining visibility." Three guards appeared from the back of the field, horses lathered from heat exhaustion. Two of the guards reached back as far as possible, gaining more leverage as they flogged the cutter's exposed back. The other guard swung his whip over his head and leaned his body forward to give his swing full force. He had customized his whip by tying knots in the leather, enhancing its painful effects.

"I have always been a hard worker. I'm no slacker!" the prisoner begged. "Oh Jesus! Oh Jesus!" he cried. The third guard made the sign of the cross before he flogged the cutter again, beating the helpless man like a beast. Desmond felt sick and disgusted; he turned away, unable to watch any longer. The cutter was doubled over with pain. "Now you all know what to expect. Get back to work," the guard said.

What troubled Desmond deeply was the guard making the sign of the cross before beating an innocent man. Was the guard appeasing a vengeful god? Did his god condone or encourage this? What god would want such a thing? But it was the very same sign of the cross Desmond made during times of doubt and fear. "Father, Son, and Holy Spirit," the Holy Trinity provided comfort and strength during dark times. "*Passio Christi, conforta me*" reminded Desmond that Christ died for his salvation. How could his tormentors share this same belief? As a guard passed by, Desmond noticed rosary prayer beads clenched tightly in his fist. He raised the beads to his mouth and kissed the crucifix before heading off to flog another innocent man.

The cutter was trying but unable to keep up the pace. Desmond watched as he worked slower and slower. He swung the cane knife with his right hand. His left arm crossed over his stomach, still doubled over in pain. He could endure the misery no longer and began crying out, "Jesus Christ, Jesus Christ!" His bare back was crisscrossed in every direction with deep cuts from the whips.

"Don't pray to Christ. Pray to the prison warden," another cutter suggested. "He's the only one that can help you now!"

The cutter seemed to find strength as he stood upright. "I can't die in this fucking field!" he said and began to swing the cane knife with great force. He raised his right arm high over his shoulder with the cane knife fully extended for greater leverage and a more powerful cut. His left foot was planted firmly as his right slightly rose, somewhat like a batter's stance. It takes three swings to cut through cane, only one to slice human flesh. His aim was perfect. The swing's momentum drove the cane knife deep into the back of his right foot, slicing the Achilles' tendon as intended. "Fuck you!" He laughed while sitting in a pool of his own blood. "Come get me, motherfuckers!" he yelled loudly, believing he had outsmarted the guards. "Thank you, Jesus!"

The same three guards who flogged the cutter earlier returned again. Two reached down and each grabbed an arm, dragging the cutter between the horses to a nearby tree. Resistance was pointless as the cutter tried to slow things down by twisting and turning his body in a useless effort to break free. The tree reminded Desmond of the oak he loved. The one he planted from an acorn and nurtured into a mighty oak. It gave him comfort and strength. This oak delivered only pain and death.

The third guard dismounted and began cracking his whip for practice, still making the sign of the cross. The cutter's right foot dragged along the ground like it was made of rubber, bouncing freely. Showing great zeal, one guard tied a short rope around the cutter's left wrist. The other guard held the cutter upright. The rope was tossed over a branch and the loose end tied around the cutter's right wrist. Sturdy and thick and low, oak branches are ideal for this task, a purpose Desmond had never dreamed. The cutter supported his weight by gripping the rope with both hands; his knees remained bent as he hung suspended by his arms. "I'm not a slave!" the cutter cried out.

"You are now!" the guard said as he kissed the rosary and cracked his whip, smiling.

After ten minutes of relentless flogging, the guard grew exhausted. He set the whip on the ground, placed his hands on his knees, and struggled to catch his breath. He motioned for the other two guards to cut the prisoner down. The cutter's lifeless body collapsed to the ground, his back nearly skinless. The three men gathered around the body, lowered their heads, and said the "Our Father." Then they dragged the body off.

Watching all this, Desmond finally gave up. "My God, why have you forsaken me?" he asked. Surprisingly, capitulation felt good; the burden of faith had been lifted. Desmond abandoned all hope and accepted the fact that he would most likely die there. His faith gone, he only wished that death would come quickly. There would be no heaven; his belief in a superstitious Christ-myth had been foolish. Like an oak tree, religion was neither good nor evil; it was a prop, used to disguise totalitarianism behind a charade of "blessed" purpose, he realized.

There was only one logical explanation as Desmond thought about the dead cutter, killed by religious murderers. A truth that organized religion successfully conspired to hide for two thousand years. If there was a "Holy Grail," this would be it. Jesus did not die for our salvation. Unable to overcome man's cruel nature, the truth of the crucifixion was that Christ died because God gave up! Man was alone and adrift, Desmond reasoned.

25

PRESIDENT SANDERS RESTRICTED CARBON emissions by using executive orders. She felt that the legislative process was too slow and complicated for "such important matters." Fossil fuel restrictions were driving up price and demand for biofuel, requiring Angola's sugarcane plantation and bio-refinery to work non-stop.

Carbon-based fuels were restricted to "protect the environment." But the Angola biofuel plant produced massive air pollution from its giant coal-burning smokestacks and water pollution from coal waste. Making matters more confusing was the fact that coal had to be shipped down the Mississippi River on giant barges from Canada, at great expense. All methods of domestic US coal mining had been prohibited for nearly two years. The largest mining areas in the US had been declared "National Parks," making them off-limits to mining forever.

Although the US Treasury was broke, the government was paying for expensive Canadian coal even when it was plentiful in Kentucky, Tennessee, and West Virginia. Canada used the extra income to fund massive forty percent annual defense appropriations increases. The American president explained this contradiction by saying, "America is making up for environmental sins of the industrial revolution. It makes no difference if other nations follow our lead. We have a debt to settle. We owe the planet more than others, because we have done more harm. This much we know! We must act decisively to meet this great environmental challenge." President Sanders outlined her plans to move America completely to a green economy based on renewable biofuel. She proposed cutting emissions by an additional eighty percent in three years and putting in place a plan to make sure we were "living up" to our obligations in a transparent manner.

Desmond worked under skies blackened by Angola coal smoke. Each morning he heard the thunderous sound of coal waste "clinkers" rattling down chutes into the Mississippi River. Nothing made sense.

"Desmond Dupree, wake up!" It was earlier than usual. "You have an appointment," the guards said. Desmond was taken out of the barracks building while the others slept. A guard on each side escorted him to a part of the prison compound he had never seen before. Afraid to look up, he kept his head down, showing little interest. The guards became impatient with Desmond's slow walk. Rather than unchaining his legs, they grabbed under his arms and lifted him along at a faster pace. "Let's go. You can't be late!" a guard said. Heavy steel doors were opened with a coded key. Desmond was told to sit. He realized something unusual. This building was air-conditioned.

"When was the last time you had a shower?" Desmond was asked by the man who came out to meet him.

"I don't remember," Desmond said.

"You smell disgusting. Come with me," he directed. He also instructed the guards to remove Desmond's leg chains. Desmond was taken down a carpeted hall and led to a shower room. He had forgotten how comforting a warm shower could be. Desmond brushed his teeth, shaved, and was given clean clothes.

Then he was escorted to a security desk. These guards were armed with nine-millimeter pistols and wore Special Forces insignia. Desmond's fingerprints were verified with an electronic scanner. He was cleared to proceed. "Good to meet you, Mr. Dupree." A man in an expensive suit was waiting. It had been so long since Desmond was called Mr. Dupree, he wasn't sure how to respond. Desmond held out his hand. The man shook it enthusiastically.

"I've wanted this meeting a long time, since I learned you were here at Angola. But these things do take time." The man explained that he had a subscription to Desmond's financial newsletter, "Prosperity," and had done very well following its suggestions. "Before losing everything!" he added sarcastically. He also explained that the governor's wife repeatedly placed her neck on the line to get him out of the cane fields. "She even had the governor call the White House! Good to have friends in high places. Glad you're still alive. Come with me," he said.

The room was a state-of-the-art commodities trading floor. One of the most sophisticated Desmond had seen. Dozens of powerful computers were flashing data from commodities markets across the world. Traders, some in prison uniforms, were handling four screens each, executing trades. "Take a look, Mr. Dupree. Tell me, what do you see?" the man asked.

Desmond was allowed to walk around. He spent a few minutes standing behind traders, observing activity, watching trading and strategy. "What do you think is going on here?" Desmond was asked again. A wrong answer and it was back to the cane fields. He knew the correct answer, but it seemed strange. "Well?" The man's patience was wearing thin.

"These computers are running advanced trading programs, algorithms, linked to markets in Hsia, Europe, and South America. They appear to be taking advantage of swift price movements in commodities," Desmond said. He also explained some detail about algorithms running complicated software using the calculus of probabilities. "I will need more time if you expect details on the calculus of all this. I only had twenty minutes to observe."

"Good enough," was the reply. "Did you notice anything unusual?"

"Yes, I noticed something immediately. I've seen many trading floors, but this one is quite unique. All of this technology is doing only one thing," Desmond said. "This is designed to create and maintain a market in only one commodity, biofuel. Most trading floors would try to profit from movements between different products within the energy complex," he explained. "For example, sell sweet crude and buy heating oil, or buy gasoline while selling heavy crude. It appears that the only purpose here is to drive up the price of biofuel while shorting other energy commodities regardless of economic logic."

He dared not say what he believed was really going on. US environmental regulation, restrictions on drilling and mining, and carbon controls were all designed to promote the use of Angola biofuel. It was the only fuel market the US government could manipulate and monopolize. All of this was designed to make money for politicians. Desmond realized it but did not say it out loud. He now slept in a dorm-type room on a small cot. Desmond once agonized over whether to buy a Maserati or Aston Martin sports car. Today, he was thrilled to have a thin mattress and worn wool blanket.

The biofuel refinery and commodity trading were a source of cash for the bankrupt country. By manipulating fuel supply on the commodities market, Angola traders were able to front-run price movements, raking in outrageous trading profits and artificially supporting the biofuel market. Government was doing the very same thing it accused Wall Street of doing. Back then President Sanders had investment bankers arrested for economic crimes against the nation. Now the bankers were forced to steal on behalf of the same government.

Desmond found humor in the hypocrisy of his situation. He sat at his new computer station and began to familiarize himself with the hardware. "It's Enron-esque around here. You must be Desmond Dupree." The middle-aged woman sitting next to Desmond reached out her hand. "I'm Vickie, Vickie Parsons," she said.

26

PRESIDENT SANDERS URGENTLY WANTED TO reach an agreement with LADO countries concerning the southwestern US. The president's goal of signing an "end of conflict, end of claims" final agreement was necessary to put unrest to an end. She offered almost everything demanded, including an official apology for America's 1848 war against Mexico. Surprisingly, LADO leadership refused the generous peace offer presented by the president. They reasoned that soon they would control the area anyway without having to make any political concessions. They called the Sanders plan a "sovereign cage."

With millions of illegal immigrants now crossing the wide-open southern US border, Latino demographic dominance was only a matter of time, accomplishing within months what American leaders had tried to prevent for decades. LADO leadership reasoned that the president's offer created "independence" but not "sovereignty." Soon President Sanders would have to deal with a Latino majority in the entire Southwest and have to coexist alongside an aggressive adversary within her own borders.

LADO demanded a return to the 1848 borders and then some, including all of: Texas, California, Nevada, Utah, Colorado, Arizona, New Mexico, and Wyoming. In the 1848 war, Mexico lost nearly two-thirds of its territory; now it wanted that back. The LADO president talked about Mexican "Manifest Destiny," a swipe at the imploding US. "Most of the great results of history are brought about by discreditable means," he said, once again mocking views commonly held in America during the Mexican-American War. "What does America have to complain about? All we want is what is rightfully ours!"

Texas was another problem for President Sanders. She foolishly underestimated the determination of the Lone Star state. Armed citizens took to the streets in large numbers, calling the president a traitor. The governor took direct command of the Texas National Guard and issued a call for Texans to defend their state. Hundreds of thousands responded. All very comfortable around firearms, many were ex-military.

The Sanders' government faced a Texas rebellion but felt that moving toward a two-state LADO-US solution as a first step would weaken the Texas opposition. After losing this first struggle, the Texas renegades would be in a weaker position to resist a final-status agreement later, she believed. But the news of Americans gathered around the Utah state capitol building, desperately clinging to helicopters, trying to get the last flight out, enraged Texans. Their state would not become another Saigon.

During the 1980s, the US Navy approached six hundred blue water ships. Now it was incapable of maintaining 115 vessels. The Norfolk Naval Air Station supported the US Fleet Forces Command for the Atlantic Ocean, Indian Ocean, the Mediterranean Sea, and Gulf of Mexico. The USS *Theodore Roosevelt* aircraft carrier battle group was based there and had been docked for the past five months. In the meantime sailors were assigned various duties around the base. They could all be reached in a moment's notice with an efficient text messaging system used for emergency situations. "CVN—Roosevelt Battle Group. All hands, report to stations. Status Urgent." The early morning tranquility of the base was disrupted as 3,800 sailors and naval officers rushed back to their ship.

At the North Island Naval Base near San Diego, sailors serving onboard the carrier USS *Tripoli* received similar orders. The plan was to pressure Mexico and LADO by positioning carrier groups on the Gulf of Mexico and Pacific coasts simultaneously. President Sanders believed a show of military determination would force LADO to the negotiating table, like the Christmas Bombings had done during the Vietnam War. But LADO was prepared to send a different message.

The Soviets gave up efforts to build maneuverable Anti-Ship Ballistic Missile (ASBM) systems years ago. They were unable to overcome the significant design challenges with the limited technology of the day. However, Hsia secretly deployed space-targeting electro-optical satellites needed to make modern ASBMs operational and deadly. In ancient times the Egyptians defeated a large fleet in the Mediterranean by ambushing them from shore with flaming arrows. Arrows would be replaced by Hsian/LADO anti-ship missiles, but the battle stratagem was unchanged. It doesn't always require a navy to repel a powerful naval force.

Hsian space-targeting satellites were feeding real-time data to ASBM silos hidden deep in the jungles of Venezuela. The confident US carriers left port and headed south. Four secret Venezuelan silos were built at the end of a fifteen-mile dirt road amid dense forests. Each missile was housed in a one-hundred-foot-deep silo protected by five feet of reinforced concrete. The *Roosevelt* group entered the Gulf of Mexico under the cover of darkness, passing close to Cuban waters. The *Tripoli* group was just south of the Baja Peninsula when the hidden reinforced concrete silo doors began to roll back, revealing the red nose cones of Hsian-designed ASBM warheads. Exhaust gases escaped from nearby vents as LADO crews began the launch sequence.

The new DF-21 ASBMs used by LADO forces were the most advanced available and capable of destroying a carrier group. Carrier-killer technology was a "game changer" and believed by LADO officials to signal the end of America's naval hegemony for good. However, these Venezuelan missiles were armed for a soft kill. LADO did not intend to sink the American carriers. They only planned to discredit and embarrass the American Navy. Carriers remained the last symbol of America's power and prestige.

Both carriers reached operational positions without LADO interference, turned in to the wind, and began preparing for flight operations. Defensive shipboard systems were on full alert, but no threats were tracked. Then US satellites detected the ASBM launches from heat generated by the fuel boosters just as the missiles cleared the Venezuelan silos. It was already too late. Time to impact was less than seventeen minutes. The National Security Advisor reached President Sanders as she was sitting down for dinner. She refused the call, claiming she needed downtime. "For Christ's sake! Can I have even a few minutes to myself?" she asked.

Four missiles were launched from the Venezuela jungle. The first two were armed with electromagnetic pulse generators and the other two with tungsten rod flechette penetrators. The pulse generators would render all electronic equipment useless. The other missile would release a flechette cluster of non-explosive, high-speed metal penetrators. The "tungsten shower" covered a three thousand square foot area and would kill unprotected crew, destroy most airplanes and anything not protected by robust armor plating. This one-two punch was expected to leave the carriers dead in the water.

The *Tripoli* was hit first. Its captain ordered evasive maneuvers and launched defensive measures designed to protect his ship, but his undisciplined crew seemed more interested in their iPods than their radar screens. He did everything by the book, including flight operations, but his efforts did not fool targeting satellites already locked on. The electromagnetic pulse weapon detonated first with a blinding flash. All electronic equipment and anything using microprocessors were instantly destroyed. The *Tripoli* battle group was defenseless, with no communications or operable weapons. The worst was yet to come.

The second warhead detonated forty-five seconds later, twenty thousand feet directly above the defenseless USS *Tripoli*. Thousands of flechettes hit the *Tripoli* at a velocity of fourteen thousand feet per second. The "tungsten shower" destroyed everything unprotected. Death rained down like a thunderstorm, violent and powerful. Bloody body parts and destroyed airplanes littered the *Tripoli's* flight deck. Watching from the safety of his armored bridge, the captain could not believe the destruction he saw. Helpless, he placed his face in his hands, unable to comprehend the death of his ship. "What have I done?" he repeated again and again. He looked up quickly enough to realize his fatal mistake. "Checkmate" was all he had time to say.

When he received the first attack warnings, the captain ordered emergency wing operations. Only one F18 was launched before the first blast. The movement of aircraft for flight operations left the armored hangar bay doors open, exposing the carrier's soft inner belly. Thousands of flechettes bounced around and penetrated the ship's internal compartments, including the nuclear reactor space, destroying its cooling system. With no way to shut down or control the damaged reactor, it reached critical in less than three minutes.

The atomic blast lit the night sky like a sunrise. A massive yellow and orange ball of superheated nuclear gases climbed above the horizon and could be seen for miles in all directions. The explosion was equivalent to the power of a limited yield battlefield nuclear warhead scoring a direct hit. At its center, temperatures were hot enough to turn steel into molten liquid. The *Tripoli* battle group disappeared.

27

REAR ADMIRAL J.M. SMITH WAS born in Texas and grew up around the East Texas oilfields. His first job was as an oilfield roughneck, working his way through Texas A&M University. The Navy ROTC program helped to cover college expenses and fulfilled his desire to give back to the country he loved. Admiral Smith earned his first command during Operation Desert Shield and Desert Storm, serving on Spruance-class destroyers. Now he was a two-star rear admiral, and the USS *Theodore Roosevelt* served as his flagship.

Admiral Smith's battle group, including two Arleigh Burke destroyers, entered the Gulf of Mexico on Alert Five and ready to fight. Anticipating trouble, he had three F18s fueled, armed, and ready to catapult off the flight deck at a moment's notice. US satellites were now tracking the incoming missiles and feeding the trajectory information directly to the *Theodore Roosevelt* group. Admiral Smith gave two orders. First he launched the three F18s. Two fighters headed for Venezuela, locked onto the missile launch locations. It was important to make sure LADO could not target the carrier group with more missiles. "Say hello to our LADO friends," Admiral Smith said over the radio as the jets headed south at Mach 1.8. The third F18 pilot jammed his throttle forward and pointed the jet's nose in a vertical climb with full afterburners, heading for an altitude of seventy thousand feet. The flight manual for the F18 claimed an altitude ceiling of sixty thousand feet plus.

"I've always wondered exactly what that 'plus' means," the pilot said as he pushed the fighter past its limits.

Admiral Smith's second order could seem counterintuitive. The expected command would have been to order evasive maneuvers according to standard procedure, like the *Tripoli* had done. "All stop!" The entire battle group came to a dead stop. His crew would crawl over broken glass for him. No one doubted or questioned the admiral's unusual order. LADO ASBMs were locked on to their targets, and no amount of zigzagging, decoys, or deception emitters would change that. At a dead stop, the Roosevelt and Arleigh Burke destroyers could more effectively target the incoming threats, actually enhancing their survival odds and giving them a fighting chance.

The electrometric pulse missile was inbound first. LADO was using the same attack plan that worked so well earlier on the *Tripoli*, but these Arleigh Burke destroyers were equipped with the Aegis Ballistic Missile Defense System. This time they were ready. Shooting down a missile was not like "hitting a bullet with a bullet." It was only necessary to put your missile in the path of the incoming enemy missile. The ASBMs used by LADO had one major advantage: Once launched, their trajectory was maneuverable. "Take them out!" Admiral Smith gave the order while standing outside of the *Roosevelt's* bridge, watching the battle unfold. The Arleigh Burkes did not disappoint.

Topside launchers swung into action, firing six intercept missiles. Each one sounded like a screaming top-fuel dragster. Admiral Smith loved the sting of battle. "Give them hell, boys!" He waved his cap wildly, showing approval to the destroyer crews.

Once the Aegis Ballistic Missile Defense system went into action, it never failed. The LADO ASBM, pulse weapon already armed, was beginning to angle down toward the *Roosevelt* group, just as predicted by the Arleigh Burke computers. It was greeted by six powerful explosions. Debris fell harmlessly into the Gulf 150 miles away from the *Roosevelt*. The flechette missile was still inbound, about forty-five seconds behind the first. Because of budget cuts the Arleigh Burkes had no more missiles to fire. Admiral Smith was not concerned.

The single F18 reached seventy thousand feet. The pilot's body strained from the negative Gs. His vision blurred as the G-forces press his eyeballs against their sockets. Under his right wing was the ASM 140. Its Exo-Atmospheric Kinetic Warhead was designed to kill satellites. "Kill Vehicle away," the pilot radioed the *Roosevelt* as the missile's thrust motors kicked in. Its thirty-one kilograms of explosives were guided to their target by the ship for a direct hit. The fragile Hsia Electro-Optical Targeting satellite broke apart, creating a small meteor shower as its pieces fell back to earth. Without guidance the last LADO ASBM circled around like a lost puppy. With fuel exhausted, it also fell harmlessly into the Gulf of Mexico. When the F18 returned, much of the paint on the fighter's nose and leading wing edges was gone, worn away by the extreme flight maneuvers. "We'll get her repainted for you, sir," the young flight technician said. "Nice flying," he added.

Back in Venezuela well-trained crews quickly prepared to fire additional missiles. When the rocket motors ignited, massive heat signatures were generated, making it easy for the infrared tracking missiles fired by the other two F18s to find their targets. Dense jungle offered false security. Sonic booms created by the two fighter jets rattled the missile base, alerting technicians to their unfortunate situation. "Greetings from the *Roosevelt*. Have a nice day!" the flight leader said as air-to-ground missiles fired from the F18s impacted the silos just as the ASBMs were lifting off. The rocket fuel ignited in massive explosions, sending flames shooting two hundred feet into the sky.

Admiral Smith turned the *Roosevelt* into the wind, beginning wing operations. His crew launched two armed fighters every twenty seconds. The *Roosevelt* used a hydraulic system to catapult planes, whereas older carriers used steam. Planes were hooked onto a track on the flight deck. When the signal was given, the catapult system launched the fighters, reaching take-off velocity in twenty-five yards. Directly below the flight deck, the hydraulic catapult mechanism went from zero to 110 miles per hour and then dead stop, all in less than one and a half seconds. A bright yellow line painted on the floor warns about standing too close. 'Probability of death' was painted in red letters.

Pilots go below the flight deck, into the catapult area. They stand with the tips of their shoes touching the yellow warning line. The massive speeding catapult mechanism stops inches from their faces, the pilots toy with death, showing no emotion. Admiral Smith salutes each pilot, "Make us proud," he said.

A group of LADO fast attack boats were detected approaching the *Roosevelt* group from the West. They do not respond to repeated warnings and close to within fifty miles of the carrier. Admiral Smith gives the order, "Time to finish this fracas. Sink the fuckers." It takes less than three hours for the Roosevelt's fighters to clear the Gulf of all LADO combat vessels. The US Navy did not forget how to fight; they just had not been unleashed.

Admiral Smith was ordered to return to homeport. "Combat operations not authorized. Cease aggressive actions immediately. Return to Norfolk." President Sanders was concerned that Admiral Smith was starting a "real shooting war." At the presidential press conference, she reaffirmed her commitment to peace and spoke about the unfortunate loss of life aboard the *Tripoli*. She promised a full investigation into the "tragic reactor accident."

Admiral Smith had never disobeyed an order, especially one directly from the president. *First time for everything*, he thought and walked over to the young sailor manning the helm. "Change our course, son."

The sailor complied. "Yes sir, setting new course, Norfolk, Virginia."

Admiral Smith looked out over the flight deck. "Make that new course for Galveston, Texas!" he said.

28

DESMOND WAS ALLOWED VERY LIMITED access
to news and current events, although being well informed was necessary to do his job trading biofuel on the world's exchanges. Besides, he
was a prisoner with limited outside contacts anyway. It made no sense
to keep him completely in the dark. News he did receive was washed
through filters and government sensors, making it worthless. He felt
like a mushroom, always kept in the dark and fed shit.

Vickie sometimes had interesting information and shared it with
Desmond. "That reactor incident on the Stennis was no accident,"
Vickie leaned over and whispered to Desmond. "It was attacked by
LADO ASBMs launched from bases hidden in the Venezuelan jungle," she said. Desmond showed no reaction to the news he already
suspected anyway. *Carriers don't blow up on their own,* he thought, *but
how could Vickie know anything about Venezuelan missiles?* "Kiss me
now, Desmond!" Vickie demanded as she caressed his inner thigh.
She leaned back toward her computers after drawing the guard's
attention. "If the guards think we're lovers, they won't be suspicious
seeing us talk. Next time kiss like you mean it. Our lives depend on
it!"

Desmond wanted to trust Vickie, but he remained suspicious. He
did not want to go back to the cane fields or worse. Vickie and
Desmond had access to the same computer systems, but somehow she
always had more information. How was that possible? Desmond

smelled a rat. He did not know that some guards were former Air Force Special Forces having served under the command of Wayne Parsons, and they remained loyal to him. These guards kept Vickie informed and had pledged to protect her. But she needed the very specialized skills of an expert investment banker like Desmond. He passed the first loyalty test by keeping quiet thus far with the tidbits of information Vickie had already shared. Time was running out; things would get dangerous from here.

Desmond implemented a Scale Trading system, initiating buy orders to support the biofuel price. Since the flow of biofuel from Angola was manipulated, he never sold contracts at a loss. He stabilized prices at constantly higher levels. His job, as a trader, was to create a price floor, preventing most downward price movement. The average price per barrel for biofuel over the last seven years was $65 to $83. Desmond set up buy orders every fifty cents price break lower— $64.50, $64.00, $63.50, etc. He was buying five thousand barrels per contract per account.

He then placed orders to sell each contract fifty cents above his original price. If the price was falling, Desmond's buy positions kicked in, reversing the downward trend. Biofuel prices always moved back up to the higher averages because President Sanders made sure they did. "The worldwide use of biofuel will continue to expand as a common-sense approach to combating climate change. Biofuel is good for consumers, the economy, our country, and our environment," she said. When President Sanders spoke, Desmond's contracts cashed out like Vegas slot machines.

President Sanders and the Federal Reserve also conspired to keep biofuel prices high by keeping the dollar cheap. The president blamed "greedy Wall Street speculators" for the abnormally high biofuel prices. To hope that biofuel would become less expensive while the currency in which it was priced continued to depreciate was economic fantasy.

Desmond always bet on rising fuel prices because he understood dollar value fundamentals. "There is no such thing as cheap or expensive fuel. There is dollar depreciation requiring more and more worthless dollars to purchase the same barrel of fuel," Desmond said to Vickie. "A barrel of bio is a barrel of bio. It never changes. The dollar's value changes constantly, affecting prices." Each contract Desmond successfully traded earned fifty cents times five thousand barrels for a twenty-five-hundred-dollar profit. He managed thousands of trades in hundreds of different accounts. It was easy money.

Many of the accounts Desmond traded were owned by the US Treasury Department, Commerce Department, or US Federal Reserve. A few very large and unusual accounts were identified numerically with activity routed around the world, over different exchanges, hiding ownership. These were the accounts Vickie was interested in. She asked Desmond if he had "found any information, anything at all?" on the encrypted accounts. "Please keep looking. This is extremely urgent," she said, knowing that Desmond was the best at this sort of thing.

Desmond had not seen or heard from Karen and Isabella since the night of his arrest. "They may be in Texas, living under the name of Garcia, Karen's maiden name," he explained to Vickie. "I left money and instructions to help them reach family in Texas. Protect my family and I'll get all the account information you want," Desmond promised. He suspected Vickie had unique influence. Vickie decided not to tell him about recent events in Texas.

29

KAREN COLLECTED A FEW POSSESSIONS from the pile of rubble that had once been home, and she located a car for sale. It happened to be a Citroen that was sold for cash, no questions asked. The seller was eager to close the deal and assured Karen the Citroen ran "like a new car."

She looked it over. "That's a weird-looking car," she said.

"It's not weird. It's French," the seller replied. Isabella said it was "ugly."

Karen hid gold coins under seats, behind the fire wall, in the trunk and engine compartment. She traveled under her maiden name, Garcia, afraid she may be linked to Desmond's arrest warrants.

Desmond owned one gun. It was a gift from a dear friend. Dr. John was a commander during World War II. He witnessed most of the Pacific war's bloodiest battles, but as a doctor, never fired his Colt .45 model 1911. The Colt was designed to knock down and kill with one shot. "Not like the little nine-millimeter popguns used today," Dr. John told Desmond. His son, David, spent the Vietnam War in Canada as a draft dodger. Disappointed in his son, Dr. John gave the .45 to Desmond.

Karen found the gun and extra clips. She wore it on her hip the way she used to carry a cell phone. Her phones and iPods had been empty status symbols. The .45 commanded respect. Just the sight of such a powerful weapon would keep trouble away, she hoped. If not, she was willing to shoot anyone who crossed her path.

During her college years Karen joined the Navy Reserves as a corpsman. The program covered tuition in exchange for a six-year commitment to one weekend of training per month. Training included marksmanship competitions using .45s. Recruits learned how to handle firearms first with a .22 that was the same weight and balance as the .45 but had no kick. Karen was rated first in her company using the small-caliber pistol. "Don't expect to do as well with the real thing," the instructor advised. He was trying to be supportive but realistic at the same time.

Karen was not intimidated. She was ready to fire the real .45 and eager to experience its thrust and power. After a short time of "getting acquainted" with a real .45, she became the best marksman in fleet competitions, winning recognitions and honors. At 105 pounds she was easy to underestimate. Mental toughness always trumps physical strength.

Karen chambered a round and slapped a clip in, giving her one extra shot. The weight of the fully loaded .45 felt comforting. She moved her arm from left to right, checking the balance. "Hello, old friend. It's been a long time," she said as she slipped the .45 into its holster. Karen and Isabella left New Orleans at night, traveling back roads, trying to stay out of sight. The Citroen's top speed was only forty-five, and it required radiator water often. At Baton Rouge they headed west toward Houston, passing a few miles from Angola, never realizing Desmond was nearby. During better times, traveling from New Orleans to Houston was a pleasant five-hour drive. The same trip would take Karen and Isabella nearly two days.

They reached the town of Slaughter west of Baton Rouge and stopped at a small roadside stand selling potatoes grown in a nearby field. "Y'all take y'alls time looking around," the woman working the stand said. Karen purchased enough potatoes to last the trip.

"Any farmers around here willing to sell bio?" Karen asked.

"You from the government?" the woman inquired with her heavy country drawl.

Karen explained that they were just trying to get home. Farmers were allowed special fuel allocations as agriculture was considered an "essential" activity. Karen assumed some farmers would be willing to sell a few gallons. "My husband works in the barn just over the hill." The woman pointed Karen in the right direction. "Gold coins only. No paper money," she said.

The Citroen was designed to run on premium unleaded, not bio-fuel. Consequently, gaskets and fuel lines deteriorated quickly, increasing fuel consumption to about eight miles per gallon. The farmer was willing to sell biofuel and moved a tractor so the Citroen could pull close to his fuel storage tank. Isabella was asleep on the backseat. The farmer walked around and around, "Where is the gas cap on this thing?" he asked.

Karen leaned over the back bumper and found a small panel near the left taillight. "Here it is!" she said.

The farmer reached around and began fondling Karen's breasts. "How about gold for the bio and some pussy for my trouble?" he asked. Karen could feel his erection and wiggled her ass from side to side, distracting him. The farmer unbuttoned Karen's pants and started to turn her around. The feel of her pubic hair caused his heart rate to increase. He closed his eyes, enjoying the anticipation.

When his eyes opened a moment later, he found the business end of the .45 an inch from his forehead. Karen's finger on the trigger was rock steady; she did not blink. "That's a fucking cannon! Good-bye, hard-on," the farmer said, pulling his pants up. Karen advised him to go back to the produce stand and screw his wife.

"She won't shoot you," Karen said.

Karen and Isabella made it to Lafayette. The Citroen was over-heating and nearly out of fuel again. She pulled to the side of the road, stopping under an oak. She turned off the engine and tried to figure things out. "Sacre bleu! Is that a Citroen?" Isabella was first to notice the man approaching from the passenger side. He spoke with a Cajun accent and the same French terms Desmond used. Karen was a good judge of people and guessed the Cajun bougalie was friendly. "I'm Thesimond. Nice to meet you," he said. She moved her finger away from the .45's trigger. "This is one fine automobile. Best car France ever made," he said excitedly.

Karen was puzzled. "Are you referring to this car?"

She explained that they were heading to Texas and had no other transportation available. "Can you fix it?" she asked. "I can pay you." Thesimond seemed to appreciate the opportunity to work on the Citroen. Karen followed him to a small house on the outskirts of town.

His wife was sitting in a rocking chair on the porch of the poorly maintained home. She offered Karen and Isabella fried catfish sandwiches while Thesimond worked under the Citroen's hood. The catfish po-boys were wonderful. *Beats eating raw potatoes again,* Karen thought. "I think my husband loves French cars more than me! But he does have nice buns," the woman said while watching Thesimond lean under the Citroen's hood. He filled the radiator, patched a leaky hose, and placed a cool, wet towel over the fuel injection system, cooling it down to normal operating temperatures.

"I can try and fix the radiator better. But don't think you can make it to Texas. The fuel injection system needs new gaskets and seals," Thesimond said, closing the hood. He carefully wiped his fingerprints off the hood as if the car were a restored classic. He walked around, admiring the car's unusual lines. "Some people say the Citroen looks like a cockroach. I think it's beautiful," he said.

"Who owns that old truck?" Karen asked. There was a rusty Chevy parked behind a shed. The couple explained that since their appliance repair business failed, they had no use for the truck. "How about an even swap? Citroen for the Chevy?" Karen suggested.

Disappointed, Thesimond said "no" politely. "The Citroen is too valuable. It's worth much more than that old truck. We don't have any money to give you," he added.

The wife spoke up. "Don't listen to him. We will take the trade. The truck looks bad, but runs great, always well maintained," she said. She liked seeing her husband excited like this. They behaved like young honeymooners. The playful affection reminded Karen of how much she missed Desmond.

Karen and Isabella moved their things to the truck and thanked the couple. Before she left, Karen placed a gift of ten gold coins on their coffee table.

The Chevy had a full tank of bio and made it past Lake Charles to the Texas/Louisiana border without incident. They waited in a short line with other cars. The guards on the Texas side asked her name. "Karen Garcia," she said. They reviewed a list and instructed Karen to pull into a parking space in a fenced-off area to the right. She was handcuffed, escorted to a temporary holding area, and placed under arrest by order of the governor of Texas. Isabella was crying but allowed to stay with Karen. The truck was searched.

30

ADMIRAL SMITH ENFORCED A "NO fly-no drive" zone around Texas with orders for his F-18s to attack and destroy any potentially hostile aircraft or ground vehicles approaching Texas. LADO armored columns were stopped cold after F-18s destroyed four tank groups moving toward the Mexican/Texas border fence. Each group contained twenty-five tanks and various support vehicles. They were heading east along a road between hills. The fighter jets destroyed the first and last tanks in each column. Trapped, the remaining tanks were doomed. Surviving crews tried to run for cover; most never made it. The road became known as "The Devil's Driveway," with burned bodies and burned-out tanks stretching over three miles.

With their borders secure, the Texas legislature and governor were free to focus on a domestic agenda, but they went too far. First they passed laws segregating police departments. Hispanic officers who were not fired were tucked away in predominantly Hispanic districts. They were required to wear plain clothes, stay out of sight from whites, and were unarmed. "Mexicans will no longer have authority over whites," the Texas governor said.

In Houston, a Mexican boy was trying to earn extra income for his family by polishing shoes. A bloated, red-faced Texas State Trooper approached the boy, calling him a "Mexican nigger." The officer confiscated the shoeshine box and pushed the boy to the ground. He dumped the box's contents onto the street and kicked the articles down a storm drain.

The boy tried to explain. "Please, mister. I'm leaving," but the trooper was worked into a fury, his face red with rage. He smashed the wooden shine box to the ground. He picked it up and smashed it to the ground again; he stomped on the pieces. In undisciplined rage he pulled his nine-millimeter pistol from its holster and pointed it at the crying boy's forehead. "Go back to Mexico where you belong. We don't want you here in Texas! Mexican bastard!" the trooper said. Kneeling, the scared boy made the sign of the cross and began praying to the Blessed Mother. "Why are all you Mexican fuckers Catholic?" the trooper asked just before pulling the trigger.

The execution was captured on a cell phone camera and viewed around the world. The Texas governor refused to discipline the officer because he was near "retirement age and had a distinguished career serving the people of Texas," he said from a hospital room while awaiting oral surgery. The governor was having four teeth extracted because he believed old fillings were causing his arthritis.

Later the Texas governor retracted the statement, claiming hospital "serum" caused his cavalier and insensitive remarks.

President Sanders said the officer was "a barbarian and a racist sadist!" She pledged to act if the Texas situation continued to deteriorate. She threatened to establish a committee to "investigate the matter," she said while promising to leave all options "on the table!"

Admiral Smith was appalled by the Texas situation and realized the governor was an embarrassment and completely out of control.

A tidal wave of segregationist legislation, including a call for a constitutional convention, made its way through a special session of Texas legislature. Any public office holder who opposed it was committing political suicide. The governor planned to use the convention to strip Mexican-American citizens of their civil rights. In a display of parliamentary maneuvers, the governor's floor leaders took control of the process and pushed a motion to suspend the rules. They forced a vote that referred the governor's legislative package directly to committee. Within five minutes 150 bills were sent to committee without discussion. The entire legislative agenda was passed by both Houses with little difficulty.

Persons of Mexican heritage unable to prove "proper" Texan citizenship could be arrested without cause. Twenty-three Mexican holding areas called "Liberty Parks" were authorized and built in remote areas around the state. "Most Mexicans favor segregation," the governor said at a press conference. A sharp-eyed reporter noticed the governor was wearing mismatched shoes, one black and one brown.

"I am proud to be the governor of all people! Separate housing for Mexicans is now embodied in the laws of the State of Texas, and I am obliged to honor it," he said. Privately he ridiculed Mexicans, calling them "spics" and "wetbacks." The governor's estranged wife claimed her husband enjoyed visiting Mexican houses of prostitution.

"He spent a hundred and fifty thousand dollars in six months on his favorite young Mexican girlfriends," she testified during divorce hearings.

"Boys will be boys," a reporter said on a nightly news program defending the governor's behavior.

Admiral Smith was watching the news that night as well. "Boys will be boys! Yes! But boys will never lead great nations," he said.

Contrary to what the governor believed, no one wanted to live in Liberty Park conditions. Streetlights and paved roads ended abruptly at the fenced edge of the "Parks." Trash collection and sewerage treatment were nonexistent. The streets were littered with garbage and waste. There were no recreational facilities or libraries or schools for the two hundred thousand Mexican children now living in the Parks. There was no official law enforcement or social services available in the Parks. There were illegal drugs, prostitution, and gang violence, which the Texas media always seemed to cover.

Karen was detained crossing the Texas border because the name Garcia appeared on a list of "Terrorist Suspicion" for likely LADO supporters. A search of her truck uncovered the .45 handgun and gold coins. Under Texas law she had three strikes: the unregistered gun, a suspicious name, and undisclosed gold. She could be held indefinitely without legal representation or court appearance. Karen was assigned to Liberty Park #14 outside Houston. It was built on land that was polluted by a former creosol plant. The area had been an EPA designated clean-up site, but decontamination work never began.

Housing in Park #14 was constructed from old cargo containers, the type used on ships and placed on truck beds at ports. The steel containers were stacked three high in ten rows stretching at least one mile. Makeshift wooden stairs provided access to the top containers. Door and window openings were cut into the container sides for ventilation, useless in the hundred-degree summer heat. On a population-per-square-foot basis, Park #14 was one of the most densely populated places on earth.

Dust was not a problem because the soil was soaked with oily residue from the old chemical plant, also making it impossible to grow anything. Light rain created standing puddles of sewer and filth since the creosol-soaked soil could not absorb runoff. Overflow from heavy thunderstorms ran down the streets like rivers, often backing up into the makeshift homes. Children played between the container rows in the same streets.

Karen was escorted to the main entrance of Park #14, her handcuffs were removed, and the gate was opened. Isabella stood by her side, holding her hand. Karen was given nothing except a "good luck" wish from a guard. "They sure are going to enjoy you!" he added while moving his hips back and forth, dry-humping the air. "Can I watch?" he asked. With no idea what to do next, Karen stood still, trying to look as tough as possible while wiping tears away. The gate slammed shut with a loud clap.

"Pour tequila on their dicks first. It's good disinfectant," the same guard yelled, speeding away. Karen was glad Isabella was too young and innocent to understand what was going on. "Those men were not very nice," Isabella said to her mom.

31

**PRESIDENT SANDERS ORDERED HER ATTOR-
NEY** general to sue the State of Texas and its governor for civil rights violations on behalf of those interned in the Parks. The US Justice Department filed a lawsuit challenging the constitutionality of Texas laws targeting immigrants. "Texas remains a part of the United States. Thus our constitution gives the federal government and courts authority to regulate all immigration matters. The nation's laws reflect a balance of national and humanitarian interest. They will be enforced," the president said. "It is obvious that these new Texas laws are designed to circumvent US Supreme Court civil rights decisions. The federal courts will knock these new laws down as unconstitutional as fast as Texas can enact them," she said.

"President Sanders is ignoring the damage to our state and the cost to our citizens. I hope she finds the moral courage to address the LADO issues before it is too late! Texans wonder if the Sanders administration really cares about secure borders when they sue a state that is only trying to protect its rightful citizens. Nine hundred thousand LADO illegals have entered Texas in the last seven months," the governor said. "Some may be looking for jobs, most are looking for trouble. I am convinced that if President Sanders takes action in opposition to these new laws, which are supported overwhelmingly by the people of Texas, she will bring more chaos and misfortune upon America's exhausted citizens."

President Sanders responded that other groups like the American Civil Union, Liberties Social Union, and the National Organization of College Professors were also challenging the Texas law as well. "Their injunctions mean nothing in Texas," the governor added.

In addition to the lawsuits, President Sanders ordered a type 212A attack submarine to the Gulf of Mexico off the western Louisiana coast. The small sub carried a crew of twenty-eight and was extremely effective in shallow waters. The hull and sail were designed with no straight lines, resulting in very low target radar echo. Its fuel cells operated at a temperature of seventy to eighty degrees Celsius, making detection with external heat sensors impossible.

The smooth Gulf floor allowed the sub to "lie down," hiding undetected in one hundred feet of water. The captain shut off engines and closed all seawater inlets, the sub becoming almost invisible to detection efforts. The tiny 212A packed a powerful punch. It was armed with six twenty-one-inch bow torpedo tubes and Harpoon anti-ship cruise missiles. The trap was set. The sub waited patiently for Admiral Smith and the *Roosevelt* to reenter Louisiana waters.

Vickie told Desmond what she knew about Karen and Isabella's internment at Park #14. She also promised that everything possible was being done to rescue his family. She assured him things would be okay. Desmond believed Vickie. He was working nonstop to identify the accounts, as she requested. He noticed a short note sent between two European commodities traders, a lucky break for Desmond.

The email was from one trader to a friend bragging about screwing a secretary one evening during a power outage. The trader secretly filmed the nasty encounter and emailed it to his friend. "I've been trying to fuck her for months. I finally wore her down," the trader bragged. The attachment originated in Belgium and seemed insignificant at first, until Desmond realized the careless sender inadvertently attached dozens of encrypted account numbers in a separate link.

Commodity trading account numbers work like credit card numbers; each set of digits represents important information, such as suitability, client net worth, nation of origin, margin allowance, and so forth. The specific numbers on this email corresponded to state-owned trading accounts for the benefit of wealthy European, LADO, and Hsian politicians. They were all profiting from Desmond's bio-fuel trading programs, indicating a worldwide web of interconnecting relationships.

The US Congress passed the Patriot Act after the September 11 attacks. The law was intended to stop funding of foreign terrorist organizations and their operations in the US. It required bankers to provide clients' most intimate financial information to the government. All this data was stored in powerful computers operated by the National Security Organization. The law was also used as a political and financial weapon of mass destruction. Once the Sanders administration declared Israel to be a terrorist state, the wealth of Israel's supporters in the US was legally seized. The confiscation of Jewish wealth under the Patriot Act was the largest financial windfall for the US Treasury since Franklin Roosevelt outlawed gold ownership and thus defaulted on US government debt denominated in gold.

The Patriot law was easily manipulated. A disgruntled husband used the Act to settle the score with his restless wife. He forged her name to a check and donated $2,500 to a Hebrew "cultural" fund. The charity was named on the State Department's terrorist watch list. The wife was arrested under the Patriot Act, spent six months in jail, and now was a registered felon. Her husband married a neighbor while she was incarcerated.

On a hunch, using a password provided by Vickie, Desmond ran the European account numbers through the massive Patriot Act data base. Desmond cross-referenced the information with associated financial relationships. The entire process took only a few seconds. "It's no wonder identity theft is such a problem. Governments make it so easy," Desmond said. The largest accounts belonged to President Sanders and members of her administration. There was even an account for the governor of Texas, the Hsian president, and many high-ranking LADO politicians.

Once Desmond decoded the encrypted accounts, it was clear President Sander's net worth was many billions of dollars. Most of her cash was held in US accounts, although some were in the form of Hsian and LADO Monetary Fund deposit guarantees. The president's cash was used to leverage additional biofuel trades and timed to benefit from government activity, creating greater and greater wealth for her and outrageous conflicts of interest.

"All this pain and suffering at Angola is only for money," Desmond said, confirming his previously held suspicions. "The entire Green movement is an elaborate hoax, perpetrated upon sheepish populations. All designed to make politicians rich. Charlatans! The world doesn't need biofuel any more than it needs windmill farms," Desmond said to Vickie. "Sanders doesn't stand up to LADO and Hsia leaders because they are all whores working the same street corner. It's a damn worldwide fraud!"

"Nice job identifying the accounts. We're ahead of schedule," Vickie said, ignoring Desmond's emotional rant. She told him that his job was not finished. "Stay calm! We need you to do more. Much more! This is the real reason you're here," she said. "You have an important role to play, a chance to change history." Vickie explained that the plan's success depended on Desmond manipulating the biofuel markets. "Do you have the balls to destroy a presidency?" she asked him.

"Yes, I'd kill Sanders myself if it guaranteed Karen and Isabella's freedom!" Desmond said.

Vickie smiled. Desmond was tougher than she expected, "her white collar warrior," she called him. She reminded Desmond again that his family would be safe. "All part of the plan," she promised.

"Desmond, you have three days to document everything possible about these accounts and Sanders' involvement. The information will be used by the Northern Alliance to encourage the formation of a new American government," Vickie said and kissed him again. The guards looked away, still assuming the two were lovers. "One more thing—

we need you to create massive losses, bankrupt every account, and strip them of every dollar!" she said. Desmond's trading programs helped create the wealth; now he was happy for the chance to take it all back.

"A square deal," Desmond called it. "Okay, but what happens in three days?" he asked.

Vickie explained that the Angola biofuel plant would be destroyed by Northern Alliance commandoes, Karen and Isabella would be extracted from Park #14, and "we can go home," she said.

32

WITHIN A FEW MOMENTS OF their arrival at Park #14, Karen and Isabella were approached by two Mexican men, one about sixteen years old, the other a grown man. They spoke perfect English. "Do you have any place to go?"

Karen and Isabella were invited to their "home," which was a first-level container shared with three other families. A mother and three young daughters welcomed them. "We don't have much, but we share. We take care of each other here," the mother said. The daughters asked Isabella to be their friend.

Dinner consisted of surplus MREs with 1990s date stamps. Karen remembered "Meals Ready to Eat" from the Navy and also from the aftermath of hurricanes on the Gulf Coast. After major storms, MREs provided by National Guard troops were the only food available for long periods.

At mealtime the families sat in a circle on the floor. The oldest man recited the "Our Father." The others bowed their heads, all holding hands. Each individual MRE was divided three ways. Before eating, each person took a moment to say what they were thankful for. "I'm thankful for this meal," a child said. "I'm thankful for my family," said another. The adults prayed for President Sanders and the Texas governor, hoping for fairness. The youngest girl asked when Danny was coming home. "I miss him." She started to cry. Karen realized from listening to the conversation that Danny was never coming home.

Danny was twelve years old and earned money for his family by polishing shoes in downtown Houston. He was shot by a drunken state trooper. The family hired a lawyer to help retrieve Danny's body for proper burial in a Catholic cemetery. The local sheriff decided the family were troublemakers and ordered their arrest and internment at Park #14. Their assets were seized by the Texas government, including homes and the family's construction business. The Mexican father was a former US Marine. They had all been US citizens since birth.

The mother hugged her young daughter. "We all miss Danny," she said.

33

COAL FOR THE ANGOLA BIOFUEL plant came from Canada. It was loaded onto barges in the Great Lakes and made its way to Chicago, where the Illinois River connected the Great Lakes to the Mississippi River. The barges passed through eight locks and dams on the Illinois River before heading down the Mississippi on river trains. The river trains consisted of numerous barges linked together and pushed by two thirty-thousand-horsepower tugboats. Each individual barge was as long as a football field, somewhat narrow and designed specifically for this task.

This unique barge design allowed river trains to pass each other heading north and south on narrow parts of the Mississippi River and fit the Illinois River locks. The excessive length of the trains required special tugboats with pilothouses raised twenty-five feet above the deck so captains could see the entire length of the floating trains. The pilothouses, perched on top of steel superstructures, resembled guard towers common around the Angola fields, appropriate considering their current use.

Eight river trains worked constantly, delivering enough coal to fuel the giant Angola bio plant. Four trains were always loaded heading south while the others headed back to Canada. The process continued around the clock, nonstop. Coal transportation had the right-of-way regarding all other river traffic, insuring that nothing interfered with coal delivery.

In an enclosed Canadian dry dock, Northern Alliance shipfitters and marine engineers secretly worked to modify two barges. They built retractable roofs and installed living compartments and hidden helicopter pads. The first barge was designed to accommodate six Apache Longbow attack helicopters and crews. The second barge was built for larger Chinook helicopters intended to transport and deploy teams of Special Ops. It had been said, "If you want new ideas, read an old book." In the 1930s the USS *Macon*, a Navy dirigible, could launch biplane fighters with a skyhook. During WWII the Japanese developed a way to install fighter planes on special submarines. In the 1980s the US Army developed a plan to place armed reconnaissance helicopters on container ships.

The commandos were former members of Mossad's Special Ops, Israel's most secret warriors. They had been described as "the dark side of a dark service." They were equally at home in the fine hotels of Europe or the dark alleys of Beirut. They tattooed their blood type on their arms, making the corpsman's job easier if battlefield attention was necessary. Some foreign intelligence services could probably identify the men as former Mossad agents, but could never prove any current Northern Alliance affiliation. They were chameleons. If anything went wrong, the Northern Alliance had plausible denial, claiming the group was a rogue remnant of former Israel Defense Forces (IDF).

The barge roofs were closed and covered with a thin layer of coal, making them look exactly like other barges. The Israeli assault commander had been arrested for flying drunk and crash-landing a helicopter. The pilot was working for a private helicopter service when he ran out of fuel and landed on a suburban street. He claimed a fuel gauge malfunctioned, but he had been flying around looking at women sun-tanning nude in the privacy of backyards. He lost track of time. News media ran with the story, claiming the once-feared Israeli Special Forces were now despondent alcoholics unable to hold down simple jobs. The entire episode was a deception orchestrated by Northern Alliance Intelligence to deflect attention from the real mission.

The "Trojan Horse" barges were quietly slipped into line. Two older barges, needing repair, were taken back in exchange, as was routine for river train operations. Thus no suspicions were raised. Colonel Parsons flew to the *Roosevelt*, undetected in his stealth F-22. Admiral Smith was waiting on the *Roosevelt's* flight deck. There was no salute; instead they embraced in a way reserved for men who survived combat together. "Great to see you, old friend," Admiral Smith said.

The *Roosevelt* battle group headed east from the Galveston/Houston area toward Louisiana. The eager captain of the 212A attack submarine quietly ordered his men to battle stations. The courageous little sub lifted off the sea floor. Orders to attack were expected once the *Roosevelt* carrier group violated Louisiana waters.

Two Super Stallion Marine Corps CH-53s were on the *Roosevelt's* flight deck, carrying Marine assault teams. Each individual Marine had the most recent photos available of Karen and Isabella. Flight time to Liberty Park #14 was thirty-five minutes.

The Super Stallions arrived over the Park at dusk and pinpointed Karen and Isabella's probable location. The container housing was strong enough to support the CH-53's weight, but the pilots hovered inches above the rooftops, unsure of their stability. The rear ramps were lowered, and heavily armed Marines scrambled out. The goal was to extract Desmond's family without wounding innocent bystanders.

The helicopters made a terrifying noise. Armed Marines were running about, demanding, "Friend or foe?" The Mexican father gathered his family together, directing them to a corner. He stood in front of them with his arms outstretched, his body between the children and the front door. "Daddy will protect you," he promised.

Karen jumped up. "They're Marines!" she said, recognizing the unique sound of Navy helicopters. The father reached for something in a small suitcase. "No!" Karen cried. "They will kill you!" But he was not reaching for a gun. It was the battle flag that flew over his base when he was a US Marine officer stationed in Beirut, Lebanon.

He draped the Marine Corp flag over his frightened children. "This will protect you," he promised.

Three young Marines, in a wedge formation, burst in. "Located objective," the group leader, Corporal Alexander "Zander" LeBlanc, said into a small transmitter built into his helmet. He held his left arm out and patted the air with his hand, signaling to the other two Marines to lower their weapons. "Located objective," he repeated. "Both are safe and with friends!"

Corporal Zander examined the battle-torn Marine Corps flag and noticed the Mexican father's tattoo: Semper Fidelis, with the letters "GCE." Every Marine knows that GCE means "ground combat element." The young Marine saluted the father. "Sir, it's always an honor to meet a fellow Marine."

"The honor is mine, son. Can you get my family out of here?" the father asked.

Corporal Zander made the call following predetermined protocol. "Marines never leave anyone behind! Semper Fi," the young Marine said.

Karen was surprised to find out the Marines were there looking for her and Isabella. She smiled. "Desmond, what have you gotten into this time?" she wondered, always believing he would find some way to protect her. Thirty-five minutes later Karen, Isabella, and the Mexican family were safe aboard the *Roosevelt's* flight deck.

"Welcome aboard, everyone," Admiral Smith said. He saluted the father. Karen learned that, if things went according to plan, she would see Desmond in a few hours.

The second Super Stallion landed nearby. Corporal Zander approached. He saluted Admiral Smith, then turned to the father. "I believe this belongs to you, sir." The father held the tattered Marine Corps flag tight against his heart. "Hell of a job!" Admiral Smith told Corporal Zander. "Hell of a job!"

34

THE *ROOSEVELT* CONTINUED TO HEAD east, closer to Louisiana waters. The captain of the 212A submarine could now see the battle group through his periscope. His well-disciplined crew quietly prepared to set their deadly trap. On board the *Roosevelt,* Colonel Parsons presented a leather case to the admiral. "I present this to you on behalf of those fighting for freedom," he said. "Hope still lives. Welcome to the good fight," the colonel said.

Admiral Smith accepted the case. "This is something I must do alone. Please understand," he said.

The *Roosevelt* was two miles from entering Louisiana waters, where it intended to make sure F15s from the Belle Chasse Naval Air Station near New Orleans did not scramble to defend Angola. The 212A captain was tracking the carrier's movement and confirming coordinates through the periscope. "My god! Stop the attack! Stand down! Stand down!" The submarine commander was panicking. "Send an emergency message now!" The first officer warned that breaking radio silence would compromise their position.

In the leather case were two flags. Admiral Smith lowered the American flag. He carefully folded it and respectfully stored it away. First he raised the new flag of the Northern Alliance. A similar flagging tactic was used successfully in the1980s when temporarily reflagged oil tankers traveling the Strait of Hormuz flew the American flag. The Iranians would not dare attack American-flagged oil tankers back then, and the Northern Alliance believed President Sanders would not attack a warship flying the flag of a nuclear-armed nation now.

The president was motivated by the need to advance her policy goals and would see only what she wanted to see based on those interests. She may have understood the seriousness of the situation but deliberately misrepresented reality in a strategic attempt to influence perceptions, including her own. She also displayed more confidence in her own biased conclusions than was warranted by available data. President Sanders' style contributed to a lack of open debate. She consciously ignored information regarding the *Roosevelt's* intentions when it did not fit her limited understanding. She reacted exactly as predicted in Northern Alliance intelligence reports.

The Gadsden flag was made famous during the American Revolution, a curled rattlesnake and a defiant motto, "Don't Tread on Me!" The *Roosevelt* was now so close to the 212A that the submarine's crew could hear cheers from sailors as the two flags were raised above the *Roosevelt*. The flag of the Northern Alliance resembled the American flag, but with some differences. It had only three stars on a blue background, representing life, liberty, and happiness. Instead of thirteen stripes, it had only three, a stripe for each branch of government, recognizing the importance of checks and balances.

As expected President Sanders was unwilling to authorize an attack on a Northern Alliance flagged warship. She did organize a meeting of her senior advisors for the next morning. Without new orders the captain of the 212A watched as the *Roosevelt* group moved harmlessly past his position toward the coastal Louisiana area, where it would play an important role in the destruction of the Angola biofuel plant.

The emergency radio transmission from the submarine exposed its position. Within moments an Arleigh Burke destroyer from the *Roosevelt* group was bearing down on the submarine's location. The shallow gulf waters presented limited defensive options, and the captain ordered his submarine to surface. He presented the vessel to the destroyer's commander and negotiated the safety of his crew. The men were removed and the submarine was scuttled.

"Every battle is won or lost before fighting ever begins," Admiral Smith said while watching developments through binoculars.

35

IT IS EASY TO MAKE the mistake of confusing investing with gambling, but there is a fundamental difference between the two: Gambling odds always favors the house. When free markets operate efficiently, no individual or entity has an inherent advantage. There is no "house" in fair markets.

President Sanders and her cronies manipulated the biofuel market for so long, they believed they were the "house." In self-assured arrogance they left free market mechanisms in place, believing they could always manipulate biofuel trading to their advantage.

Desmond viewed market swings as trading opportunities. He could make money in any down or up market. In down markets he "shorted" key companies. Desmond borrowed shares from brokerage firms and sold them on the open market. When he sold five hundred borrowed shares of Caterpillar at $50, he raised $25,000. The key here was that Desmond had to replace five hundred Caterpillar shares, not the $25,000. He waited three weeks, and by then the shares were trading at $35. Five hundred shares at $35 cost $17,500. Desmond replaced the five hundred borrowed shares and made $7,500 profit on the trade.

In quiet markets he made money selling "calls." Desmond granted other investors the contractual right to buy his shares at a predetermined price at some specific time in the future. They paid for that right. If the stock did not reach the "strike price," then Desmond kept his stock and the cash he received for selling the "call." If the stock went up, then Desmond had to deliver stock at the agreed-upon price. He only sold "calls" when he was certain the stock would stay the same or drop. Desmond loved taking advantage of other investors when they made foolish judgments.

On special occasions Desmond sold calls uncovered. In these trades he was absolutely sure the stock would stay in the expected range. He collected cash for selling the calls, and if the stock did not go up, then Desmond kept the premium as profit without risking any of his own cash. However, his risk was unlimited because the stock could go up indefinitely. Desmond would have to buy highly appreciated shares on the open market and sell them to the call buyer at the lower agreed prices. Entire fortunes have been lost trading uncovered options. Desmond only did this type of risky investing when he had access to privileged information. He remembered what the HADA-COL specialist said on the floor of the exchange all those years ago: "Forget about calculus and B-school bullshit. Information is the only thing of any real value." The fact that the world's largest biofuel facility would soon be destroyed was the best inside information anyone ever had.

President Sanders had no major environmental issues on the agenda except a conference planned for late summer. When Desmond started repositioning accounts, it did not draw concern because no one expected any short-term biofuel price movement. He sold calls both covered and uncovered. Lazy traders around the world mirrored his positions, generating massive amounts of cash during quiet trading sessions and creating unlimited leveraged liability as well. Any sudden biofuel price shock would completely destroy account values.

Desmond took the other side of the trades by secretly buying calls. He routed the trades through the over-sexed and unfocused broker in Belgium. Desmond hacked into his amateurish system. It was as easy as stealing wireless Internet from a neighbor. "Why miss an opportunity to make money for myself? I deserve it," Desmond reasoned.

Since Angola was the only source for most biofuel, inventory of the fuel in storage was always limited. There simply was not enough to go around, and limited supply equals higher prices. As with any commodity, low inventories means price shocks can be fast and violent.

Desmond's Belgium trades went unnoticed because he invested in the old carbon-based fuels: crude oil, diesel, and gasoline. Heavy call activity in these markets were under the radar because no one paid attention to "obsolete" fuels anymore. Like driving a Ford Model T on an interstate highway, they just thought he was nuts. But Desmond knew that once the supply of biofuel was disrupted, prices for other fuels would skyrocket—making him a wealthy man and bankrupting corrupt politicians in the bargain.

It was a perfect setup, supported by corrupt governments and over-confident, lazy traders piggy-backing Desmond's playbook. Vickie asked why he looked so happy. "If you don't know who the mark is, it's probably you," Desmond said as he entered more trades. He tapped out "Easy Living" by Uriah Heep with the fingers of his left hand as his right hand worked the keyboard like a philharmonic conductor.

"My white collar warrior," Vickie said with a wink and friendly pat on his knee.

T.S. Eliot said that life is a grand journey, but eventually we all end up back where we started. Desmond was convinced otherwise. Faith could be terrifying, like a cane field, where life was spent hiding from dangerous men on horseback. Desmond deserted his faith and thought he would never go back to the superstitious "Christ myth" he once cherished. "If I'm going to be dead forever, I might as well make the most of living now, right?" Desmond asked Vickie sarcastically as he entered the last trades.

She rolled her eyes toward the ceiling, questioning his assessment. "Forever is an awful long time," she said.

36

WHILE THE RIVER TRAIN WAS tying up at the Angola dock, deckhands tossed heavy ropes from the barges to crews dressed in brown uniforms and orange caps. Ropes were secured to giant cleats and tightened down as the tugboats maneuvered into position. The coal-unloading process had become routine for the undisciplined guards; most sat around smoking cigarettes or shooting dice. Their weapons were lying around haphazardly.

An alert member of the dock crew noticed something unusual. "Look how high those two barges are riding!" Although they appeared to be fully loaded with coal, they sat at least two feet above the water-line. "That's weird," he said to the man next to him while he pulled on dock ropes.

"How the fuck would you know how a barge is supposed to float? Dumb ass!" the other man said without looking. The barge roofs were designed to open completely in fifteen seconds. High-speed electric motors kicked in, creating an unusually high-pitched sound that caught everyone's attention.

The massive roof panels were automatically raised on metal tracks, then lowered along the barge sides, opening like giant clamshells. Immediately after the roof panels were clear, helicopter blades were locked into place, and the General Electric turboshaft engines spooled up. The Apache gunships rose from deep within the belly of the barges like angry beasts, spitting death and destruction in all directions.

Ground assault troops swarmed from the barges. They used camouflage makeup, putting dark shades on light-skinned areas and light shades on darker facial features, creating an almost inhuman look. A similar tactic was used by Roman cavalry, who wore bronze face masks to hide all emotion. Most guards on the dock area raised their hands high in the air, trying to surrender, while others ran. Many were killed in the opening exchange. There was no plan to take prisoners. The assault teams included explosive experts placing C-4 explosives in carefully selected locations around the refining and biofuel storage areas.

The Apache Longbows led the offensive from there, killing anyone wearing a guard's uniform. They circled the cane fields first, using guards on horseback for target practice. Whips, horses, and shotguns were no match for the deadly, effective killer helicopters. Apache pilots could slave the thirty-millimeter automatic chain guns to their helmets. The guns followed the pilots' head movements. "Look at this crazy Wild Bill fucker!" the lead pilot said.

In an open field near an oak tree, a defiant guard was rearing his horse up while swinging a whip wildly above his head. He held a shotgun in the other hand, firing into the air. The reins were held in his mouth. "Let's see what happens when this crazy fucker picks on someone his own size," the lead pilot said. A half-second firing of the chain gun was enough. The guard's body dissolved into a bloody mess. He died a few feet from the same oak tree he used to hang cutters from. His blood mixed with theirs as it trickled into Angola's rich soil. The Apache Longbows moved on, destroying the guard's barracks, headquarters building, and armory.

Fighters from the Belle Chasse Naval Air Station near New Orleans scrambled to defend Angola. Flight crews worked frantically, trying to ready obsolete F14s for combat. Brave pilots sat in the cockpits, eager to join the fight, but arming fighters on short notice takes time. Most ammunition and other weapons were stored in the ordinance depot on the other side of the airfield. Only the base commander had the entry codes. But he had left early, planning a "date night" with his young wife.

The first group of five F18s from the *Roosevelt* did a low flyover above the still unarmed F14s, hoping the show of force would help avoid the destruction of the historic Belle Chasse field and save lives. "Look at that!" an excited sergeant said while pointing at the approaching F18s. "Look at that! Under their wings!" The bottom of each F18 wing was painted with the defiant curled rattlesnake, Don't Tread on Me. "They're from the *Roosevelt!*" Men on the ground began to cheer and pump their fists in the air.

Back at Angola, sounds of explosions reach the bio trading building with reports of dozens of guards killed by an unknown force that appeared from nowhere. Guards were running about in panic, most stripping off their uniforms; no one was paying any attention to Vickie or Desmond. "Why would anyone attack this shit hole?" one guard asked another as they ran for the exits.

Desmond let his finger hover over the "send" key on his computer keyboard. Vickie held her hand over his, and they pressed the key together. "Giddy up!" Desmond said. He had secretly built a list of the world's leading news organizations and opposition governments in Hsia and LADO countries, opposition leaders in the US Congress and Supreme Court, freedom fighters in Eastern Europe, and NGO groups around the world. The list included over twenty thousand names of the world's most influential individuals and organizations.

The email contained detailed descriptions of biofuel price manipulation and account documents with specific names, including a spreadsheet showing the massive kickbacks given to corrupt politicians. Every trade over the last six months was tied back to President Sanders as the money was dispersed around the world. "Time to go home, Desmond!" Vickie said, just as giant Chinook helicopters landed nearby.

The building doors swung open, and two guards appeared with submachine guns. They got down on one knee, raised their guns to firing position, and quickly scanned the room. "Vickie and Desmond, let's go! Now!" the first guard demanded in an urgent tone. These two were members of the secret team of double agents who had protected Vickie. Desmond and Vickie followed the guards down the main corridor toward the exits, running as they stepped over numerous dead bodies littering the floor. Desmond slipped in a pool of blood. On the ground next to him was a dead guard lying face down. On the guard's right arm was a tattoo of the Liberty Bell. Desmond grabbed the guard's hair and raised his head. As a reward for his loyalty, Beer Boy was given a "good" job at Angola. Desmond enjoyed the irony of the situation for a moment, got up, and continued running. Many guards were killed by liberated prisoners. They picked up weapons from dead guards and were rampaging across the Angola complex, seeking revenge.

Desmond and Vickie were met by a second team setting up a defensive perimeter around the helicopter landing area. As soon as they were aboard, the first Chinook helicopter headed south, toward the *Roosevelt*. The other Chinooks follow close behind, escorted by F18s from the *Roosevelt*. Moments later the helicopters began to shake violently as powerful shock waves hit. One helicopter was brought down by debris from the exploding biofuel plant.

Vickie sat close to Desmond, extending her right arm across the top of his seat. He rested his head against her arm, "Angola was hell," she said, "but perhaps the cane fields were more hellish because you gave up. When you faced despair, what pulled you through? When deep in hell's inner circle, what saved you? Maybe God had been protecting you all along, Desmond. You may have given up on him, but I don't think God ever lost faith in you." Desmond was more inclined to trust Vickie than God. "But people, especially trusted friends, can disappoint," she reminded him. Perhaps Vickie was right. Was God with him all along? he wondered.

Desmond stared from the open helicopter window and considered what Vickie said, watching explosions fading into the distance. He didn't regret not sleeping with her, although she was very attractive. His thoughts had always been with Karen.

The violence of Angola gave way to a clear night sky. Lights from the *Roosevelt's* flight deck appeared in the distance, reflecting off the water's peaceful surface. Soon Desmond would be reunited with his family and safe inside Northern Alliance borders.

Karen and Desmond had been married a long time, although physical passion had long since cooled, replaced by an inseparable commitment to each other. Their occasional sex was still exciting and eagerly anticipated, "like honey on the stinger," Desmond liked to say. It was a fulfilling desire most couples never experienced because they gave up too easily. Overlooking pain caused by youthful misjudgment was difficult, but the rewards of lifelong passion were worth the emotional risk, Desmond reasoned. He had learned that the passage of time eased even the most hurtful memories, leaving jealousy and anger to wither away in insignificance. Karen and Isabella ran into his arms as he stepped from the helicopter onto the *Roosevelt's* flight deck.

37

DESMOND, KAREN, AND ISABELLA WERE
brought to Toronto; they were expecting to go to Alaska, but the
Northern Alliance learned of Desmond's love for trains and arranged
for them to travel the Canadian National Railway back to Alaska.
Desmond enjoyed the glass observation car, especially riding through
the Canadian Rockies. Stories about Angola were everywhere on the
Internet. Most major newspapers ran first-page stories. Desmond had
become somewhat of a celebrity and received calls from numerous
world leaders.

His cell phone rang. "It's the French ambassador!" Desmond said
to Karen. "He wants to know if the new French government can do
anything for us!" Karen asked for the phone. The ambassador was surprised by the unusual nature of her request, but he promised to personally handle it. Karen wished she could have been in Lafayette to
see Thesimond's reaction to the new Citroen delivered by official representatives of the French government! Sacre bleu!

Money was not an issue, as Desmond's oil and coal investments
did very well. Maturity taught Desmond that bad times never last forever; unfortunately, neither do the good. But he was surprised at how
quickly things can change. President Sanders denied any knowledge
or involvement in the biofuel price fixing scandal. She blamed everything on "one unsupervised rogue Wall Street trader," she said. "He
orchestrated Angola's destruction for his own personal financial gain."

She promised investigations to ferret out this "financial wrecking ball and bring him to justice!"

With Angola destroyed, the American biofuel-based economy sank further into depression. A desperate President Sanders reluctantly signed expensive carbon-based energy agreements with the Northern Alliance. Demand for coal, gasoline, and crude oil was making the Northern Alliance a wealthy nation. The environmental movement and biofuel industry suffered a devastating setback as the world turned back toward carbon fuels, exactly as Desmond expected.

The US Congress appointed a special prosecutor with a team of experienced investigators to prosecute the Angola matter. Vickie was named a person of interest, but was offered immunity in exchange for testimony against Desmond. She was represented by Northern Alliance lawyers and diplomats interested in building stronger commercial ties with the American government by opening new markets for Canada's abundant energy resources.

"A simple 'yes' to the following questions will be sufficient for our purposes at this time," the American prosecutor said to Vickie. "Did Desmond Dupree design and implement computer programs used to manipulate the biofuel trading market? Yes or no?" he asked.

"Did Desmond Dupree profit personally from inside information regarding the timing of Angola's destruction and carbon fuel price appreciation? Yes or no?" he asked.

The prosecutor asked questions only when he was sure of the answers, but he needed confirmation from Vickie for the indictments. "Yes or no will be sufficient. Please answer," he said. After a short consultation with the Alliance lawyers, Vickie nodded her head confidently. "Yes," she said. The prosecutor began collecting his papers. "You have been quite helpful, Mrs. Parsons, thank you." He left the room.

On the strength of Vickie's testimony, Northern Alliance diplomats agreed to turn Desmond over to US authorities. Leaders from both countries proclaimed a new era of friendship and economic cooperation. Desmond had already been arrested by Northern Alliance agents and was in a van with blacked-out windows; his hands were cuffed, and his legs were shackled together with a short steel chain, making it impossible for him to run. Northern Alliance authorities walked him over to their side of the border checkpoint. Desmond shuffled along, taking very small steps. Fifty yards away American security agents waited on their side of the border.

Vickie stood nearby. "Sorry," she said and turned away. He harbored no bitterness toward her, but he wondered if he had slept with her, would things have turned out differently? Desmond was good at unraveling the tapestry of political intrigue and realized that like Vickie, he was an expendable pawn stuck between powerful forces. Desmond's new imprisonment meant the Northern Alliance would sell a lot of oil, President Sanders would win reelection, and Karen and Isabella were safe. Everyone won with Desmond taking the fall. His religious faith was now completely gone and his faith in loyalty broken by Vickie's betrayal, but he would be okay. Karen stood nearby, tears in her eyes.

A gentle breeze caught Desmond's attention. It reminded him of his dad's station wagon, driving along the highway on a cool night with the windows down. His dad drove with his left hand on the wheel and his right arm extended across the top of the front seat. Desmond's head rested against his dad's arm. A preacher on AM radio played in the background, trying to save souls. As a boy, he loved watching stars from the car window, dreaming of good things. Desmond's mind could still be someplace else, someplace better.

The American agents put Desmond in a helicopter and flew south toward New York. They landed near the outskirts of the city and transferred Desmond to a black Suburban SUV. They drove a short distance, stopping at a small park surrounded by a group of federal buildings. Desmond noticed a single oak with branches that reached skyward, then arched back to the ground. It was in the center of the square.

Desmond was escorted toward the court building with guards on each side. He looked back again. He knew this place. It was the same park where he had fallen in love with Grace all those years before. "Move along," a federal agent demanded. Desmond pretended to trip. Before getting up he clenched an acorn and held it tight. "What do you have in your hand?" the agent demanded, pulling Desmond's fingers open. Desmond resisted with all his strength. "Open your hand!" he demanded again. "It's only an acorn. A goddamn acorn," the guard said to the other agents. "It's only a damn acorn!"